THE MAKING SENSE OF THINGS

More Praise for *The Making Sense of Things*

"George Choundas writes with wit, precision, and near-eerie acuity. In one of these wondrous stories, a dog is 'marking the territory of loss,' which is what Choundas himself is doing (rather more gracefully) throughout, traversing love and aloneness in its many forms. These are stories that linger and burn."

—**Dawn Raffel**, author of *The Secret Life of Objects*

"These stories are wildly touching, funny in really funny ways, but also flights of mind, image, fantasy, and language telling us that reality is as malleable as love and as changeable as a fire in a forest."

—**G. K. Wuori**, author of *HoneyLee's Girl*

"At first I thought that George Choundas was going a long way out of the way in order to come back a short distance correctly. I read on, though, and I realized that despite their simplicity, these stories were delivering a terrific wallop.

He's working around the language, working to take it back. 'Words alone are certain good,' Yeats wrote, but words are no longer ours. Words have become the property of advertisers, corporate and political sloganeers. George Choundas is taking back the mother tongue. It's a bit of a shock now that we've become accustomed to language as the medium in which false intimacy is traded for real cash. Turns out though that we can still write to one another and write beautifully about love and death.

God Bless George Choundas and his lonely work."

—**Benjamin H. Cheever**

"George Choundas in *The Making Sense of Things* plucks the chords of string theory like a parallaxing Hermes at home in every single dimension devised. Each entry is a portal that captures all the alternate stars out of the corners of our depth-delivering eyes."

—**Michael Martone**, author of *Michael Martone*
and *Winesburg, Indiana*

THE MAKING SENSE OF THINGS

GEORGE CHOUNDAS

FC2

TUSCALOOSA

FC2 is an imprint of The University of Alabama Press
Inquiries about reproducing material from this work should be
addressed to The University of Alabama Press

Book Design: Publications Unit, Department of English, Illinois State
    University; Director: Steve Halle, Production Assistant: Charley
    Koenig
Cover Design: Lou Robinson
Typeface: Garamond

Library of Congress Cataloging-in-Publication Data

Names: Choundas, George, author.
Title: The making sense of things / George Choundas.
Description: Tuscaloosa : FC2, [2018]
Identifiers: LCCN 2017041268 (print) | LCCN 2017051058 (ebook) |
ISBN
  9781573668767 (ebook) | ISBN 9781573660655 (softcover) | ISBN
  9781573668767 (e-isbn)
Classification: LCC PS3603.H69 (ebook) | LCC PS3603.H69 A6 2018
(print) | DDC
  813/.6--dc23
LC record available at https://lccn.loc.gov/2017041268

To Adis, the maker of the happening of things.
And to Panagiotis, the maker of
the making sense of things.

CONTENTS

THE MAKING SENSE OF THINGS

TROTH

IT WAS A WORLD EXACTLY LIKE OURS, WITH THREE DIFFERENCES.

First, short went first. When two people crossed paths, the taller gave the right of way. Same if they reached a door at the same time. Or bumped into each other.

The rule was simple. Even children learned "sky hangs, earth moves" and fumbled past each other in reverse height order. The rule was logical. A taller person could better view and anticipate a crossing situation, then make up lost time with longer strides. With time the rule became custom. It reigned in all cultures, including those where in this world ladies go first, and where the reverse is true, and where age bestows priority, and where strangers' shoulder caps are things for sudden nuzzling because no convention adheres.

The time saved in any given encounter was small. Multiplied across the other world's bus stops and vestibules and elevators, it saved days and months. It happens that nine lurching dances of uncertainty in a hallway contain enough moments for a breakthrough in the arts or sciences.

The other world was globalizing as relentlessly as ours. The rule accomplished there what the jagged heap of customs in our world cannot. Take for instance the Walloon, the Yemenite, and the Aleutian Islander who converge on the same entrance to the duty-free shop in Charles de Gaulle's Terminal 2A–the narrow entrance, the one to the side. In our world they are destined each to lose three seconds picking at the floor with sheepish feet and blinking. Four, if a mixed-gender assortment. In the other world they moved around each other like breezes in a courtyard.

There was another benefit. Persons equipped to navigate physical encounters with ease and poise, even without common language, could not help but feel better about almost everything. There was nourishment in repeatedly confronting a problem, one so fleshy and immediate, and solving it instantly. A steady drip of these small but sure successes made people think of their souls as places where good things happened, rather than sticks that chafed against life's corners.

The other world, in sum, was more accomplished, more fulfilled. It was a better world.

He shows up late. The groom strolls over and thanks him for arriving before the couple's first child. They join the other groomsmen.

At the front a priest speaks instructions to the church's ceiling.

Across the nave stand the bridesmaids. They loom around the bride. She is a tiny woman with nervous looks and perfume that wears like a shriek. Except when speaking, she offers her friends only the sides of her head.

When it comes time to rehearse the procession, both groups filter into the nave and make their way back toward the entrance.

He first sees her when she stops. This bridesmaid has paused to let a short groomsman pass. She waits with her head at a kind tilt. She resembles someone hoping everything will turn out all right.

She first sees him when the rehearsal is over. He is waiting to use the restroom off the narthex, yawning.

Second, people had two hearts. Each. One heart took the same place in the body as yours or mine. Were one a doctor, or a fitness trainer anxious to suggest erudition, or the kind of person who has attended an auction of ancient maps, one called it the upper heart. Otherwise it was known as the high heart. Like hearts in this world, the high heart enjoyed the shelter of a rib cage. The low heart, and there will be no surprise in this, sat lower in the abdomen. It also had four chambers, but was smaller. It wore the liver like a sun hat.

A second heart was the fruit of evolution. In the state of nature, torpor is death. In the other world, too many early humans had fallen asleep after meals, their blood wicked away from brains by working stomachs. Too many had woken up bleary and confused, under trees, outside caves, aware for a weird instant that their heads had turned into agonies and these agonies had a color and this color was specific but oddly indefinite, either stabbing red or crushing black. Too many survived just short of realizing that ravaging jaws meant both.

A stray mutation changed everything. After a large meal the low heart could dedicate itself to the viscera. This freed the high heart to keep the brain alert as an indignant bird.

The evolutionary advantage was significant. The two-hearted were better nourished for not having to choose between eating well and staying safe. They were less vulnerable to attack, and so lived longer, and so procreated often and saw their offspring through adolescence.

The two-hearted quickly established themselves as the dominant line. The one-hearted fought off sleep but not extinction.

Popular myth doted over the two hearts. Many believed the caged heart an animal, lurching against its bars, responsible for the passions: fury, revulsion, brutality, righteousness, elation. The low heart, on the other hand, was a jewel that needed plushness and velvetry to protect it. So it glinted quietly: pride, regret, resentment, sympathy, contentment. In certain traditions the high heart stoked new love, while out of the low one leached the serene affection of couples with grown children and a preference for sitting side by side while dining. In others the low heart discharged prudent love, the kind that revels in cheerful, circumspect, adequately insured spouses, while the high heart craved velocity and calamity and ex-convicts with darling white teeth.

It was generally accepted that the high heart, from its vantage, gazed into the future, while the low heart mired itself in the past.

People in the other world lived longer. They were more awake to life as they lived it. It was a better world.

The hotel room is warm. She likes this. Maybe it will incubate boldness in her.

She sits cross-legged, shoes off. The panty-hosed toe of the suspended foot dips like a bashful eyelash.

He sits on the end of the bed, bow tie loosened. He watches her face. She takes him in with glances.

You seem like a calm person, she says. The way she holds the wineglass exposes as much web between fingers as possible.

I am a calm person, he says.

Really? You don't let anything get to you.

Not usually.

She puts down her wine and leans over.

Let's see. She places a hand on his high heart. So slow.

I exercise.

What about this one? she says, slipping her hand down to his low heart. This one doesn't lie.

He man-giggles, chuffing twice through his nose with his mouth closed.

It lies less, he says.

I know something that doesn't lie, she says. Her hand waits a sly moment.

Yes, he thinks, but it spits when it talks. You're beautiful, he says.

Third, there was *troth*. There existed in every language a word that meant *both*, except for three things, not two. In English the term was *troth*. In Spanish it was *trambos*. In Tuvan, *yшелзэ*.

It was a small thing. *Thrice* is a triplish word. Terms like *all* and *everything* can refer to three things. Or five, or fifteen. An inessential word like *troth* should not have mattered.

But it did.

Perhaps it was because troth was so concrete. All and everything are abstractions. They flap out of the mouth and alight where they will. Troth grabbed with three hands:

"Still, sparkling, or tap?"

"Troth, thank you."

"Go to the last verse. Good strong voice, now."

"'I will troth lay me down in peace, and sleep, and dream: for thou, Lord, only makest me dwell in safety.'"

"A car? With what money are you getting a car? You crying to your mother again? Or maybe you'll sell your blood, like before. Maybe the rest of you."

"Maybe troth. Maybe go fuck yourself."

Perhaps it was because troth brought things together. The word did not simply point, like *thrice*. It gathered. It tied things up with a common twine, conveyed them in a single bindle of a truth. Or perhaps it was because troth seemed like pure surfeit. It forked over both choices and the compromise to boot. It promised a union more populous than even love could manage. It spoke to each who spoke the word of possibility.

Or perhaps it was the peace it gave. In this world, we feel our hearts thumping every waking moment. Even with our single hearts, we feel a double beat: bip, bup. This two-tick, this I-am iamb, is in fact the sound of life until death—the bip heedless, the bup cowed and watchful. It is the footfall of a cripple, hobbled by the knowledge that one day he will not exist.

Those in the other world, who thought more possible, who lived in threes as much as twos, did not feel the same beat. Even when the hearts worked in unison, and made the same rhythm as in our world, the result was different.

Bip-bup-bip was the cadence of experience, the first and last moments vital and lancing, the middle a pale slurry. Bup-bip-bup traced the substance of experience: the wandering contemplation of what something might be like; the abrupt punch of it while you're barely looking; the trailing memory of it thinning out to randomnesses—the dumb extrovert smell of new plastic, a caved-in voice, yellows.

Troth took the sound of dying and made it the noise of living.

The other world brimmed with potential. Life was expansive, hopeful, defiant. It was a better world.

He frowns sometimes. It is the same frown people make when they crane down looking for lint on their shoulders. Their third dinner, she realizes he does this when he is trying to remember something.

She has a fascinating aspect. It is not her heterogeneous body, its panther parts and its pudding parts, or her skin's smell like sun-cooked windowpane. Their third time, he realizes it is that she does not know where to put her eyes.

In the other world, the short-goes-first rule had one exception. A woman carrying a child went first. Always. It did not matter how tall she was, or if she carried the child in her arms or in her womb. Conspicuously pregnant women moved about as if the planet were abandoned.

This exception was observed as assiduously as the rule. Many contended this was no exception, only rigorous compliance. Babies, whether shucked or pupating, were always shorter.

The exception did not work when child-burdened

women crossed paths. These encounters reverted to short-goes-first. Women tended to allow priority not to the smaller woman, however, but to the woman with the smaller child. This started as a small mischief, warm and sisterly and subversive, but ripened into tradition. Pregnant women delighted—or pretended delight, if they were tired or in a rush—in comparing bellies.

Sometimes two persons of the same height crossed paths. For this there was no rule. A solution had to be improvised. Often one person extended a tentative or reassuring or flamboyant palm and let the other go first. Usually this worked. But sometimes the lettee resented this, suspecting the lettor believed himself taller. His resentment was not of the gesture, but of what it seemed to reflect. What, after all, might lead someone, absent visible evidence, to assume he was taller or the other shorter? An arrogance so powerful it warped his sense of his own dimension? A contemptuous judgment of some aspect of the lettee—his clothing or his carriage or his complexion, his resemblance to some miscreant—that in a subconscious instant diminished the stature the lettor believed the lettee could credibly possess? Whatever it was, the lettee was often sure he did not like it. The lettor, for his part, routinely cautioned himself not to expect thanks but found himself searching the lettee anyway for the slightest acknowledgment—an amiable jut of the lower lip, a conscientious tuck of the head, a shifting of weight toe-ward to telegraph a quickening gait—and always, always begrudged its absence.

The other solution, of course, was for one person simply to forge ahead. This approach (best taken after meeting eyes or trading grins or otherwise signaling mutually an imminent collision) was perhaps the most expedient. It also spared the nonforger the suggestion he was obviously shorter. But the nonforger sometimes took this the wrong way. He thought the forger too ready to favor himself. He bristled at the kind of conceit that could spawn such self-advantaging. These projected antipathies addled like a two-tined serving fork in the underbrain. Meanwhile the forger, outwardly all bluff efficacy, engaged inwardly in his own self-torment. He perked his ears up as he put his head down to pass, daring himself to hear the exaggerated shuff of shoes coming to an impatient stop.

Ethnic differences heated the forkpoints to glowing. Certain populations were taller than others. Encounters between their members happened often in this other globalizing world, most without consequence. But repeated encounters between height-disparate groups planted bad seeds. Ethnic Austrians were one and a half inches taller than Turks, on average. A guest worker and serial lettee from Istanbul might wonder after a fourth tight, waiting Viennese smile whether it was the product of the gray matter perched behind it rendering him an ignorant misogynist. Three and a half inches meant that a Finn late for an appointment at Siltasaarenkatu 18 might puzzle over why he subsidized with his irretrievable time the Somalis who had failed to consult him before arriving to throng his city's sidewalks. Seven inches caused Indonesians in Amsterdam to bustle past as hastily and unobtrusively as possible, which might be viewed as smug entitlement, felt as degrading infantilization, and experienced all around as absurd and inequitable.

The biggest problem, however, was hunkering. Those

in a hurry sometimes curved their backs and compressed their necks and trained their eyes on the ground. The posture shrank them, and the averted eyes let them avoid (or claim to avoid) seeing and thus having to stop and wait for other human beings. It was a double license to untrammeled movement. The trouble with hunkering, of course, was the very plague the crossing rule prevented—collisions. Hunkerers mostly got around fine, but from time to time crashed spectacularly into shorter persons who had not guessed the rule would be ignored. Sometimes they smashed into other hunkerers: a game of chicken gone gamy. A double-hunker smashup seemed like sweet justice, but in fact it fired people's imagination so powerfully that they were prepared to believe every hunker-caused crash was a double-hunker. This in turn stigmatized the undersized and innocent victims of single-hunkers as hunkers themselves. The slightest slighted.

Cross-ethnic double-hunkers between pregnant women were rare. But when they happened, there sometimes was violence.

It is a stupid thing to do. But there is a gland, perhaps part of a heart, that urges it.

They are not married, let alone thinking about a family. Yet they name their unborn children. There will be John, after the church where they met. And Sarah and Peter, after the bride and groom who brought them together.

Sarah's life is a hard one if troth are boys, he says.

If troth are boys we have bigger troubles, she says.

With you, he says, troubles are adventures.

One day he comes home and finds her in tears.

She does not make perfect sense. She explains, tries, how this love terrifies her, how suddenly they have so much to lose.

He holds her. He tells her he knows, because he has felt these things, too. He teases her—if love upsets you, devotion will kill you—and holds her closer. She makes wet noises that are laughter. He is bending down. Before he knows what he is doing, he licks the tears off her cheeks.

He'll never be able to do that again, she thinks. At least not without making light of this moment, this wonderful moment.

He holds her some more.

They don't taste like adventure, he thinks.

Usually, the two hearts beat together. But not always. Under stress, the hearts abandoned their bicardia, their unison, and scrambled into different rhythms, dicardia, each heart for itself. Someone waiting in a crowded room to give a speech, or seeing ajar a door she locked a minute ago, or kissing for the first time a friend's lips, felt her heartsbeat not only accelerate but also diverge. Dicardia intensified nearly every emotion. Imagine the core of you launching into separate tumults. We in this world feel urgency, desperation, when our insides thrum faster. Those in the other world felt these things, too, but moreover catastrophe, or rapture, when their insides split apart.

Because the high heart sat off to the left and the low to the right, a state of excitement felt like being cracked into quarters. Limbs seemed to snap off in conspiracy with these phantom dicardiac fourths, and so a person might feel helpless or out of control, rodeo-oxed from his own exploded trunk. Oddly, a person might also feel stronger. Suddenly he sensed two power plants pulsing forcefully and independently inside him. The more the heartsbeat diverged, the more he felt strong as two men. It seemed as if he had a life to spare.

Many believed dicardia meant something more. Many believed that when a person's two hearts started beating separately, he had left the present moment. He was stalking the future (excitedly, anxiously, dreadingly), causing his high heart to race ahead, or roaming the past with his low heart (miserably, remorsefully, longingly). In either case, his one heart moved with purpose and the other straggled, like siblings on a drugstore errand.

Some referred to dicardia as being cleft and quartered. Others called it the soul going in all four of God's directions.

He knows not to make it a spectacle. They've already seen it done.

On their fall trip, just after getting coffee: they stopped at the outdoor skating rink abutting the café and watched. A few moved gorgeously. Others scraped forward and stared down as if to prop themselves up by the eyes. The rink cleared then, just two people near the center, doing what? Moving slowly, stammering with their feet really, then at a dead stop. Suddenly the man down on one knee, the girl stoppering her nostrils with the back of her hand, the onlookers putting a good face on exile with claps and hoots.

For the spring trip he suggests somewhere else. But she wants to go back. If she knew his plans, she'd insist all the more. He copes by referring sourly to the flight's connection in a different city as a compromise.

You never like change, he says.

And if that changed I wouldn't like it, she says.

They go back. Same hotel even. While she showers he visits the same café, makes arrangements with the manager, who cannot stop grinning.

Later, he comes back with her. While she looks for a table near the rink, he orders and hands it off.

A barista—so tall his apron could be a tablecloth—stops her brusquely: Ma'am, you dropped this. Would have been better with a woman, he thinks.

She says, Um, I don't think so, that's not mine.

As planned, the employee says, Oh, my mistake, tosses the ring box on the ground. Maybe harder than necessary. Walks away.

He moves toward the ring box, and kneels down to get it. She approaches. He launches into it.

Her hearts tear away from her. She stoppers her nostrils with the back of her hand. The same hand he adorns.

Back at the hotel, on the plane home, and for a day and a month short of a year, they like to stop suddenly and say, You dropped this, and kiss each other's faces.

Perhaps if she had just said, What? and taken it, all of life would be different. Perhaps in an exciting moment she would have pocketed it and urged him in a whisper to start walking. Perhaps they would have huddled together and, like people on an adventure, wondered to each other what to do.

In the other world, troth scattered possibility like pollen. It denatured death and drained off the exigency of things and replaced right and wrong with depending.

Roads and thoughts languished in disrepair.

Surgeons who placked down hard hallways toward

waiting kin felt free to plunge their hands in their pockets and express puzzlement over what to say, or to acknowledge it could have gone better.

Depictions of Justice showed her blindfolded and holding not a scale but an abacus.

There were whole traditions of art and song built around indifferent love—not the act of falling madly in it, or of sprawling heartsbroken out of it, but of loitering in it shin-deep, of musing that it is something but maybe after all simply likely not enough.

In the other world it was possible to be free of fault and still to blame.

Lately he has been quiet, and gone to bed early. It must be work. It is keeping him busy. He has pulled two all-nighters in a week.

Tonight he is still quieter. Something wrong? she asks after dinner.

Leave something alone, he says. It's everything's fault. He winks and starts for the bedroom. She starts to say, You dropped this, but he looks tired.

The next evening she comes home. There is a phone message from Sarah. Since the wedding they have spoken a couple of times. He sees Sarah more. He has kept in touch with Peter.

She enters the bedroom to change. It is different. Cleaner? She opens the closet. None of his clothes are there. She turns around. His things are gone.

She goes over the room a second time. Perhaps she is wrong. No. All gone. Except the photograph. The two of them in front of the rink. There they still are, on his bedside table, not looking at the camera. They look into each other's eyes, as if that will prop them up.

It cannot be.

She calls back. Sarah has learned it from Peter and wants to make sure she is all right. This is what Sarah says. None of it makes sense, it makes no sense at all. Sarah is kind, but the only thing Sarah can do is to say, which Sarah does, Let me know if there is anything I can do. There is nothing to do. But she does not grasp this, really is not thinking clearly, and so she is sorrowful, fatuous, wretched when she says it, slowly, because her crying mouth forms words like it is bleeding them. What can I do? Tell me? What is there I can do?

Later she will feel fury and shame and fury for having spoken those things to that woman.

Snake.

Whore.

After hearing the stories, she cannot bear to remember saying those weak things.

Sometimes, in the other world, an expectant mother felt the beat of her baby's hearts inside her. As in this world, it happened rarely, but it happened. No cynical explanation or medical condescension could contradict this. It was not the mother's own pulse. It was not indigestion. A mother knew what she felt.

And what she felt, almost always, was a single beat. The amniotic sac formed a contained environment. Rarely did anything interrupt the fetal bicardia. Silk threads and spinster aunts and fetal heartsbeats and little else were at the same time so delicate and so reliable. The beat ticked like a feather at an open window, lighter than the breeze that whispered it back and forth and back and forth.

But sometimes life intruded. Sometimes a mother grew

anxious or frightened or angry. She'd feel her own heartsbeat diverge.

Moments later, she'd feel a pair of twitchings. Two feathers. It was the baby, sharing distress it did not understand.

For a mother, this was pure anguish. It felt as if she had taken an axe to her own child.

And because life proceeds as it does, this sometimes happened more than once during a pregnancy. And the second, and third, and fourth times, as the mother grew anxious or frightened or angry, she'd realize what was to come. It was a miserable space, that lag of moments wherein the baby's single beat still prevailed, and the tiny hearts clutched obliviously to their unison, and the mother braced herself and felt blackest dread and reddest guilt and waited in the solemn company of troth heartsbeats.

Desperate, she'd think about how small her child's hearts were, how immune by virtue of sheer tininess, to things so large and coarse as her emotions. Or she'd think about all the tissuey fluid that enveloped them, really a whole ocean around two chance and crimson oysters. Sometimes these thoughts helped. Sometimes they didn't. Sometimes she hoped so hard that the strenuousness of the hoping was what pried her baby's hearts apart.

Perhaps this was evolution's work. Perhaps it was nature's calculation that a mother learn, though she'd try until death to prevent it, that it was a certainty her child would know pain, her child would know suffering, and, no matter how she tried, she could not protect it. Even mothers who thought it a lesson too cruel, who saw a distinction between causing their own babies harm and standing witness as they grew older, understood in the end they might be free of fault but still to blame.

A mother, after all, gave life.

It was troth a better world, and a worse, and our world exactly.

Five years and much has changed. Her husband is an accountant with a barrel chest. Her two sons have her looks and his appetite. She works four days a week. Three days she empties her shoes of puffed rice and sandbox.

They have never taken a trip. Weekend jaunts in the car, yes, but no planes or trains or proper suitcases. She and her husband resolve, as if it were exercise, or dental hygiene, to travel somewhere. He researches destinations. She arranges passports.

The passport office smells like cardboard, but stronger, like someone is baking it. Things are crowded but orderly. Those behind the counter make professional-grade efforts at gruffness. As she leaves the office, and crosses the building lobby, she is distracted. She riffles through her papers as she walks. At the building's main door she pushes instead of pulls. The door nudges back. It is a couple entering. She makes way.

And then. Her hearts know. They are in open revolt.

The couple's faces line up like planets, his hovering above hers. She falters to the side in four pieces. The small woman hunkers past nervously and trails perfume. She has smelled it before, and she will smell it again, elsewhere, on others. Each time it will remind her of a feeling like the opposite of nostalgia, inward and loathing, and of the daughter she almost had, of whom he never learned: the first thing to grow inside her, to make her low heart a high heart, whom she damned, when she was young and glib and useless, with a name that did not belong.

As she exits, her sheaf of papers goes loose and sheds a bit. The man picks up troth pages and holds them out to her, frowning. She tries to look down as she accepts them, and fails. Perhaps, like his wife, he does not recognize her. Sky hangs, earth moves, and perhaps he does not remember.

94 SELVAGE STREET #1

IN 1992 MY FATHER HAD A TENANT, IN HIS THIRTIES, FRIENDLY, with AIDS. He wore a sheepish smile that said he did not love himself too much. His man and cotenant left after five years. Three months later my father found fat yellow flies in the apartment and the tenant sitting on one end of the sofa. Under and around him was a silhouette of pink foam. The ambulance came. A paramedic with a clipboard walked in and said, "Uh-uh. No, sir," and walked out. A different ambulance came, took the body, and left. My father went to Kash n' Karry, bought five jugs of bleach, and poured it wherever putting down newspaper and baking soda seemed precious. He hired a Cuban who went by Jesse, and Jesse's crew of Salvadorans who went by their actual names, and paid them $200 to work the place. A half-hour later, the silhouette was gone. The pink, the clean glasses in the rack, the answering machine reading zero. All of it gone. He'd died young, and left no mark, on that long couch mostly empty.

HOW HÉCTOR VANQUISHED THE GREEKS

IN PUERTO CABELLO, VENEZUELA, THERE IS A TWELVE-YEAR-OLD boy who puts a *balón de fútbol* on the point of his left shoe. Not on the top of the foot, not against the shin. On the exact point of his shoe, like a globe on a needle. He can balance it there for ten minutes. His name is Severino. Severino can do the same on his right shoe—and leaves the ball there *indefinitely*. Even better: he can launch that ball, once balanced, with the same force as if he'd kicked it, but with more precision. It is a devastating skill.

Severino's eight-year-old brother, Héctor, can't do any of that. He envies his older brother in a way his parents have persuaded themselves is healthy and natural. He spends hours each day perfecting a different *fútbol* technique, a prodigious number of hours his parents have decided to decide is also healthy and natural because they have too many other things to worry about. Severino pays little attention to any of this because a four-year difference means whatever attention is paid to a younger sibling must be paid over the shoulder.

After weeks of practice, Héctor finally unleashes his secret skill. He does this one afternoon after school, on the field next to the used car lot, during a neighborhood game. His team lags by three points. His teammates are experiencing the kind of desperation that sucks the luck from every effort. The ball comes to Héctor. In a smooth rush of movement that boy falls to the ground, tucks the ball into the crook of his left leg, wraps his right leg around it, and his torso too, then rolls like a beetle down the field with the ball safely ensconced—not once touching the ball with his hands—and scores a goal. The neighborhood boys are astounded. A few dismiss it as gimmicky, unfair. Interestingly these critics are all on the other team. And even they want to learn how. Héctor is happy to demonstrate, over and over. Sometimes he scores by unraveling at the last moment and punching the ball with his right foot through the grasping crook of his left leg. He manages to do this from the ground, without stopping, without even slowing. But more often he scores simply by continuing to roll with his cargo through the goalposts. The latter method eliminates the risk of error, renders obsolete the very notion of defense, and is just rousing to watch. Rarely in life is the most expedient thing also the most magnificent. In this sense Héctor's roll-into-goal method is a bit of a miracle, and while the neighborhood boys are not aware this is the reason for the chills down their spines—they are still boys, so do not yet know everything—they certainly apprehend the extraordinariness of what they're witnessing.

Through all of this, Severino toes the grass, quiet. Héctor notices. How could he not?

On Saturday the boys ride the bed of Luichi's father's pickup truck down to the port, as they do every Saturday. There's room down the middle for one boy to stretch out in princely comfort; whoever gets the pleasure has to play goal when they get there. (They have not yet guessed that Tuto Fanuto only pretends to dislike playing goal.) The field down by the port has regulation-size netted goals, not stubby poles in the ground. Plus the boys get to play on a single team against all comers. Often their opponents are seamen, merchant mariners on shore leave from the freighters. The seamen, keen with land plans, glad as much for the carefreedom as for the competition, never have the right clothes on. They play in shirts that button. They play in pants that greave the length of the leg.

The Norwegians, who do not sweat, like nonetheless to untuck their shirts. The boys never lose against the Norwegians.

The Filipinos sweat plenty—their armpits grow dark beards, and the resulting Janus faces on their shirt flanks are maybe why the midfielders are so formidable—but not an untucked shirt among them. The boys sometimes lose against the Filipinos, sometimes win.

The Greeks are their grimmest adversaries. They have never beaten them. The Greeks are their favorite adversaries. The Greeks play hard, never charitably like the Filipinos. They keep intent on victory, insensible to the boys' youth, with never a suggestion that the boys are anything less than worthy competitors.

This Saturday, it's a vessel from Cardiff by way of Tampa. Carrying multifoil insulation and pneumatic drills. And Greeks.

The boys on offense charge with a raucous shouting, like cranes ashriek. The defenders hang back, sheep waiting to be milked, distantly bleating in sequence the names of teammates who happen to touch the ball.

The Greeks advance in silence.

It's 0–0 for the longest time. The Greeks are indefatigable. The boys grow restless. "Dále, Héctor!" the boys are saying. "Dále!"

Héctor gains possession. He deploys. He drops to the ground, wraps himself around the ball—more tightly than ever—and flows down the field, around the legs of two stunned Greek defenders, straight into the goal. The Greek goalkeeper stands to one side, pointing a bladed hand at Héctor and gazing upfield and asking with his whole body, "Τι είναι αυτό?"–"What is this?"–half-flummoxed and half-indignant.

The Greeks grumble, they put their eyebrows farther down than usual, but they do not protest. The boys understand the Greeks will not malign their own potency by acknowledging this trivial prank is the least concerning. And so Héctor persists. One goal after another. The boys are celebrating loudly and conspicuously between goals. After the third goal, the cheers acquire a note of jeer, and the boys—bored of embracing each other—begin to goad the opposition in the nervous oblique manner (more volume, for instance, than eye contact) of irascible puppies. And if you were on the sideline, you'd be thinking it, too: *You boys need to cut it out. You boys can't carry on like this and not get yours.*

And whether it is because fate arrives finally to right things, or because the Greeks, being Greeks, are built to out-clever the clever, a solution is hit upon. The Greeks simply start kicking Héctor as if he himself were the ball. Not in a frankly injurious way. But in a rigorous, unyielding, manhandly way. The first time he feels an unfriendly foot, Héctor, alarmed, immediately unwinds himself and springs up and loses the ball to the Greeks and their momentum-shifting goal. Severino, furious for his brother, punches one of the seamen—aiming for the chin but missing and landing sloppy on a shoulder—and storms off the field. But Héctor finds his perseverance, stays tucked against all assaults, tolerates especially the counterkicks of his teammates, who are doing their best on defense, and rumbles on. Héctor becomes the ball. Héctor is the ball.

In the end, with Severino on the sideline after having doubled back to watch—how could he not?—and dancing two-fisted and shouting "Dále, maldita tortuga mordedora, dále!" ("Go, you goddamn snapping turtle, go!"), with the Greek goalie thoroughly scandalized and staring saucer-eyed every which way in a kind of craze—the boys win.

Seven to five.

Because the other thing is, and in the neighborhood this is no secret, Héctor bites.

PLEASANTVILLE

In Pleasantville, in the first week of September, a madness sets in: autumn. Squirrels overrun porches to harass the stray nut. Raccoons bustle in quivering ovoids, prevented from fealty to any one route by the urgency of all others. Crickets know something's about to end; they misunderstand, and think it's them, and so announce themselves day and night. Panic means flight, and flight means roadkill, and the roads are lengths of black bone erupting everywhere in soft red rot.

Woodpeckers, for their part, claim the lintels and dormers and eaves. What they crave most is a place under the angled meeting of two rooflines. If these can nestle, they reason, why can't we? They perch for hours at a time, peck staunchly at these historic homes. The pecking is scandalous. The birds work two houses away and you're certain a judge and his gavel have convened court atop your kitchen ceiling. The damage is real. A single peck, though undetectable from street level, suffices to remove paint. Three pecks: a gouge easily observable to the passerby who happens to look up and certainly to Mrs. Oldmixon, whose craning and peering are the essence of her walks because her walks are one part nosiness and two parts being nosy.

In the autumn when I was twelve years old, Pleasantville had its particular ways of dealing with the woodpeckers. I don't know what ways it had before that autumn; before age twelve, I was a coil of spastic and oblivious cartilage. I do know what ways it had after that autumn. They were decidedly not the same ways, for reasons you'll soon and surely appreciate.

First way: the homeowners made a point of referring to the birds as "peckers." Unsurprisingly this disparagement did nothing to address the problem. Like clapping at the birds, like whistling and banging trash can lids and blasting air horns at the birds, like turning a hose on the birds (these were the second through sixth ways, the sixth being DJ Holt's idea, and the first and last time he executed thereon, the Hardins and the Parases and the Ketchums and the Scarozzas and the Lanes all came out to watch, also the Gibsons, but though they silently wished Holt well, they stopped short of getting their hopes up or cheering him on, careful to remind themselves this was at best a partial solution, because even if it chased away it could never deter altogether, and in the end even these restrained expectations were catastrophically dashed, because the birds did not leave, and instead took flight and circled just out of reach of the spray and brazenly replaced themselves so soon as Holt let the stream die down, and no matter how many times he surged it up again or, with surprising frequency, made contact with the brutes, they simply went aloft and waited him out and returned, and finally Holt, looking as if determined to chew one of his own molars to bits, dropped the flaccid hose where he stood and disappeared into his house, in the same direction from which, moments later—just after the birds, comfortably reroosted, delivered an especially resounding peck—came the sound of something crashing not accidentally), it didn't work.

You, reader, know the power of language. It will not surprise you that, if anything, the name-calling proved counterproductive. The birds had always annoyed. But now that they were "peckers," they were flapping sacks of affront. The calumny inflamed frustrations and stoked a jingoism that enabled these events, which, in retrospect, seem outlandish.

Rich McCabe talked hooded falcon for a solid month.

"You walk a falcon along Bedford Road, okay, those peckers are gone and they come back never."

But he made some calls (this in the days before one could simply navigate to wingeddeathdirect.com and consult the FAQ page), learned the price tag for a respectably trained specimen hovered in the thousands of dollars, and never talked hooded falcon again.

Seventh way: the homeowners armed their sons (and two daughters) with slingshots. This was precipitous, perhaps, but not heedless. The parents also dispensed instructions to always use pebbles, never rocks, to not let fly while any human stood between the slinger's nine o'clock and three o'clock, and—because the line of windows just below where the birds liked to congregate had done nothing wrong—to err on the side of missing high.

Days, then a week, and the kids hit not a single wood-pecker. The birds were wily and agile and, between pecks, unfailingly alert to danger from beneath.

Days, then a week, and the kids scared off not a single woodpecker. Inadvertently, their parents had battle-hardened these birds. It was this generation's first inheritance: a flock of trouble trained in recalcitrance, startle-proofed and inured to threat.

Single pebbles had about the same effect as oxygen. The kids learned to launch two pebbles at a time. Twin pebbles missed just as often, but occasionally they perturbed. When a bird yielded perch, the kids gave shout and celebrated. When a bird fluttered and flailed, if only for a few moments, you'd think someone's mother had brought out a tray of parfaits.

But to everything there's a dark side, and this was no exception. The kids, cowed by the novelty of sanctioned weaponry, worked peaceably together for a good three days. Like the explorers of history, they were daunted into cooperation by the unknown. By day four, however, they were arguing. This was inevitable, perhaps, not only for the campaign fatigue, but also for the forced proximity. Rather than spread themselves thin, the birds liked to mass on two or three houses at a time when actively pecking. This was a barn raising in reverse. And so the kids massed correspondingly, and conflict leached—as always it does—from the stretch and strain of finite resources. They competed for target time, and defamed each other's ability in a covert bid to secure more target time, and exhorted each other to just get out of the way.

"You're doing it wrong."

"Stay out of my nine and three."

"You're doing it wrong."

Most of the kids did the obvious thing and aimed at the birds. Orrin Androtti derided that method as hopeless. He insisted they should aim instead at the place on the house where the scatter of peck marks was most concentrated.

"That doesn't make sense, Orrin."

"You don't make sense, Shires."

It was to the boys' credit that Orrin Androtti didn't exert more influence over them than he did. A boy Orrin's size typically wields disproportionate power among his peers. He wasn't much taller than the other boys, but girthwise he rivaled most of their fathers: pork roast arms, chest like a laundry hamper. Also, his shoes were adult size thirteen. The autumn before, when Orrin wore a mere adult size eleven, the boys learned during neighborhood football games that he could not be tackled (two-hand touch was for babies) from the knees up because those feet were like prop stands. You had to go for his ankles and cinch them up. He hadn't started shaving, but by six years old his arms and legs showed bristle, and by eight his nostrils caught up, each a little vase arrangement of looping fur. Rumor was he had done something with Mrs. Cowen, the bus driver who always wore a green plaid skirt—notable among other reasons because on a public school bus it was the one article of clothing that the actual schoolgirls never wore—and Vivian Estrada, whose mother was dropping her off late to school after a doctor's appointment, actually saw Orrin and Mrs. Cowen stepping down together from an empty bus, Mrs. Cowen *stepping down first*, and Orrin was cagey about what he had done with her, which of course was the solemnest confirmation it had been everything.

Orrin was no brighter than he was tall. Paul Shires was right: Orrin's targeting approach made no sense. There might have been logic to aiming where the notches were densest had the birds been hovering while making them, and shifting randomly and quickly from hover to hover. But these were not hummingbirds. These were woodpeckers. Invariably they perched in fixed positions as they pecked. To aim at no bird was to aim at exactly nothing.

So it was pure fluke when, one Saturday, Orrin was the first not only to hit a woodpecker but to kill it. It was at the O'Rourkes' house where four birds had been perching for a day and a half. The felled bird hadn't moved in reaction to Orrin's pebble, but rather just before, or perhaps simultaneous with, its launching, and had shifted into what it couldn't have guessed was that pebble's trajectory. The bird dropped onto the ground and stayed there. It rested with its beak open, the way a bird might when barely alive and struggling quietly. This bird, however, was obviously and undoubtedly dead. What did Orrin do? He picked up a pebble (people in Pleasantville like to say it was the very same that had killed the bird, but that's lore and not fact, and so I won't pretend to report it here) and placed it in the bird's mouth. Orrin surely acted out of impulse, but looking back on it now, it strikes me as perverse the suggestion that this small creature's life, the sum total of all its struggles and perseverances, amounted to that prize in its beak: a negligible and useless rock.

That night was unusual. Typically the birds saved their pecking for daytime. But at three in the morning the pecking was so relentless at the Androttis' house that Chrissy Androtti, Orrin's mother, padded outside with a flashlight to see what was going on. (Mike Androtti, a county commissioner, was away on a business trip. There were stories that the only real business he had outside of Pleasantville was a woman in Yorktown, but everybody knew the stories were fabrications spread by Lily Sears in weird retaliation for the holiday party years ago at the Bernards' when she exceeded her recommended nightly allowance and stood and looked up at Mike Androtti with a superfluous drink in her hand and snatched at his chest with four fingers of the other as if smoothing out his sweater, but saying each time, "I like you," people noticing, and Mike grateful to see Bob Sears and saying "Bob, I think someone needs you," his eyes indicating amiably but desperately the woman still snatching at him, the relief in his face evaporating on seeing Bob just stand there with the little crowd of guests watching, standing there and holding his drink, and looking at his wife with elsewhere eyes—you know, dead eyes, eyes with no shine to them at all, because though they're apparently focused on something in the here and now, they're in fact looking elsewhere, and in Bob's case they were surveying the past and going, *No surprises here*, and they were glimpsing the future and going, *Good, fine, the more shame sowed, the more humiliation harvested*—and Lily still snatching like a kitty and still liking Mike aloud, and Mike finally resorting to a bear hug and less asking than proclaiming "Where's that mistletoe when you need it" and laughing loud with his mouth but not his eyes and hug-moving her sideways in a kind of bear-crab hybrid motion over to her husband and absconding to the relative safety of the Bernards' kitchen. There were too many claws out that night—feline, ursine, cancrine—for it not to have left a scratch on the memory of everybody in Pleasantville.) Chrissy saw nothing, a furtive rush of wings was all, before she turned back inside.

But early the next morning Chrissy and the Dabrowskis and the Ralstons were gathered outside the Androtti house, gazing up, because what they saw was unprecedented. There were no birds around. But they had left behind a pattern. A picture, really. The birds had pecked out, there above the dormer window of the house, a circle. It was an *O*. And underneath this *O* they had pecked out two short lines, as if meant to support the *O*.

This image was very clearly rendered. Depending where you looked above that dormer window, there were either great densities of marks or there were no marks at all. This was its most striking feature. Because great precision, of course, implied great purpose.

By mid-morning the grown-ups had gotten their fill, and the Androttis' curtilage was now dominated by gaping boys. The youngest, Garrett Thornwood—no relation to the town of Thornwood—was a boy who spent his Saturdays at the local library reading the kinds of books that do not circulate: morocco-bound tomes that contained secrets and pronouncements and none of the drudge in between, that spat dust into readers' faces as the price for the privilege. Sundays, on the other hand, he'd go collecting: gneiss and schist and amphibolite. Construction sites were his main game: fresh-cut ground was a loamy promise that generations of collectors hadn't already plucked out all the good rock. He was done with garnet. In his life he'd encountered four specimens: one on the far side of Opperman's Pond; one in the parking lot behind Jean-Jacques (surely this was no natural occurrence, surely some hapless child in nervous anticipation of the world's finest French toast had dropped it, and Garrett tried not to think about that and instead trained his guilty mind on the lots of people he supposed would be more than happy to trade a garnet for exceptional French toast); and two in the railbed just north of the Metro-North station platform, where he knew he shouldn't go, where he knew he'd get into serious trouble if he was caught, even though he went only on weekends when trains were few and timed his hops down from the platform onto the railbed to match one of the six times each weekend when there was a twenty-six-minute stretch with no trains passing either way. Of course, all the risk and the effort had made the garnet more precious than diamond. But garnet was a child's concern, and so was milky quartz—forget milky quartz, he could build a garage for a compact car out of all the milky quartz he'd accumulated—and he liked collecting because of the stones themselves, of course, but also because he'd been doing it for long enough that when he did it, he felt mature, and strong, and veteranly, sure of himself and of what he was doing.

His favorite: norite gabbro (pyroxene and plagioclase feldspar, Mohs hardness of 6, luster dull to submetallic). In part because Sunday afternoons were when he did his best collecting and norite gabbro looked exactly like what Sunday afternoons felt like: pleasant but cheerless, mottled, a mix of fun and clouds. In part because the name of the rock sounded like the name of someone special. Special not in a big-hug-from-Grandma kind of way; special in a badass, get-the-f-out-of-here-for-he-does-contain-too-much-awesomeness kind of way. *The name is Gabbro. Norite Gabbro.* Perhaps Gabbro adventured with a sidekick named for muscovite mica (potassium aluminum silicate hydroxide fluoride, also known as potash mica, Mohs hardness of 2 to 2.5, luster vitreous to pearly) who spoke in an extreme Russian accent. Perhaps they were long-lost brothers raised apart in far-flung sections of the world, but who later joined forces against boredom and evil, with the start of every episode depicting Muscovite "Potash" Mica all up in a lather to kill someone who had crossed them and brandishing some obsolete and garish weapon favored only by tundric nomads, and Gabbro knowing exactly what First World words of restraint and civilization (murmured in a sonorous baritone) would calm his loyal but twitchy brother and explaining why perhaps that was not a good idea in light of all that happened and still might happen, and so getting all the necessary exposition out of the way in the most comic-book-and-fantasy-adventure-loving-demographic-friendly fashion possible.

It went without saying that Gabbro and Potash kicked much ass.

Lately Garrett had reformed himself and was avoiding the railbed and sticking to the construction sites around town. Garrett's mother was not crazy about the construction sites. But she knew the shoulders of roads also beckoned (she did not know about the railbed, God help Garrett if she ever found out about the railbed, even Garrett's big brother Kevin kind of freaked out and wouldn't let up when Garrett told him about the railbed after miscalculating that Kevin would be cool about it) and so she secured promises that he would not enter any site posted for no trespassing; he would not climb over, under, or through fences; and he would not touch any form of machinery.

But some Sundays, Garrett left the rocks alone and ran with the older boys. He didn't do this often. Nor did he have a consistent reason. Once it was because in the early part of the afternoon he'd found nothing but conglomerate and more conglomerate, and to make it interesting rather than frustrating, he had imagined that the clasts—dense, insidious, adulterating—were the warts of the rock world, rampant and infectious, but after a while the conceit grew too vivid and stuck in his mind and flourished there and each time he put his fingertips on a specimen it seemed obvious that the nearest clast was sending tendrils into his phalange bones, and that conglomeration was inevitable, and that resistance was futile.

Once it was because it started to rain, and rain meant grayness and mud, which meant the finding was hard and the searching was hard, and the way the older boys ran wild made it seem like a great time and put the rain on notice that nobody gave a crap about it.

Garrett could rove with the bigger boys because his older brother Kevin was, for the past year more or less, friends with Orrin. Garrett's first few Sundays with the older boys repaid with the fleeting but intense pleasure of novelty (later not so novel, but stake out a role for yourself and inevitably you fill that role, in youth as surely as in adulthood) and Garrett justified his remora status by fetching cans of Lipton Iced Tea for the other boys from the refrigerator that Byron's grandfather kept on the screened-in back porch.

So the boys stood that morning in a jumble at the Androttis' staring up at that pecker picture, long enough that a few had floated ideas about what it looked like, dullard ideas, but not so long that the shoving that invariably erupts in a jumble of boys had yet broken out.

That's when Garrett said the pattern looked like an omega.

"Carrot says what?" said Todd Schrader.

"An omega," said Garrett.

"What's an omega?"

"Last letter of the Greek alphabet," Garrett said. "It looks like an omega. Except it's got no ankles."

"Hey, Parrot," said Bobby Minton. "Isn't your dog named Mega?"

Garrett could have said, *I don't have a dog.* But Garrett was no idiot, not in the library and not in the schoolyard, and certainly not when hearing it from punks like Bobby Minton. So he said nothing.

Bobby said, "Yeah, you got a dog named Mega, and every night you're like, 'Oh, Mega! Oh, Mega!'" and Bobby with disturbing bravura pantomimed what was meant to be Garrett squatting behind a dog, hips bucking and neck twisting, eyes shut and mouth writhing.

This was typical. This was the special savagery of the half-formed male. This was why Loretta and Ellen Sheridan, who also had slingshots, preferred to work alone.

"Bobby, don't hurt yourself," said Kevin, Garrett's brother.

"Maybe I'll hurt *you*," said Bobby to Kevin, which was just dumb because Kevin was a head taller and no joke.

"Okay," said Kevin. "Now you got two assignments. Don't hurt yourself, and don't be a fucking fuckwad."

Were there other occasions, ones in which Kevin did not intervene on his brother's behalf? Were there times when Garrett might as well have not had a brother? Like when the boys took turns hurtling on their skateboards down the long decline of the country club's entry road, during that era when the membership director still ventured out to investigate before the era when he didn't bother and just called the police right off the bat, and when Parkinson—which is what Jamie McCabe, Rich McCabe's son, liked to call Garrett when he skateboarded, for all the jerking and jittering he did to keep his balance and, self-defeatingly, his dignity—wiped out with a spectacular upflailing of limbs, and Orrin, in a feint at commiseration, brushed the mulch off Garrett's jacket with one hand and then grabbed Garrett by the hair with the other and asked, "Do you like yourself?" and seeing Garrett nod rigidly (Garrett laboring against the grip on his hair, Kevin saying nothing, Garrett looking only more plaintive for attempting stolidity) paused a moment, and grimaced, and asked, "Why?" And tossed Garrett's head aside like something to wash up after. Yes, but this is a specific story that I'm telling and I'm not getting into that.

Bobby did not react. He noted he had no audience and decided he did not need to. Instead he joined the other boys, who still gazed up at the pecker marks. The boys crowded there, all fuss and fidget.

Through all of this Orrin hadn't said anything. He hadn't said a word despite the fact that the other boys, stranded in suburbia and eager to make their own excitement, were whispering that the *O* was for Orrin, that the two pecks underneath were Orrin's giant feet, and that the birds had it out for him.

"Here they come," said Todd Schrader. One woodpecker, then two more, alighted on the Androttis' house.

Still Orrin said nothing. This is what he did instead: he bent down, and grabbed a handful of pebbles, and threw them hard enough to reach the highest parts of the house. A couple of boys tried doing the same thing, but they failed, lacking the arm to clear the second story, let alone threaten the roof. This gave Orrin the wrong kind of confidence, and once, twice, he demonstrated and cleared even the roofline with his barrage of handshot. On his third go, he abandoned his professed method of aiming at nothing, and instead aimed at an actual bird, which perched on the peak of the dormer, and one of the pebbles appeared to nip the bird's wing. This set the bird to flight, and Orrin to laughter, and the boys to jubilation, but Garrett kept silent as he watched the bird settle into a wide and descending and accelerating loop, starting roughly at the boys' one o'clock and continuing counterclockwise through their nine o'clock and gliding lower and lower through their six o'clock and at four o'clock the bird suddenly cut in toward Orrin's head and dug its two feet into his cheek and pecked once, just once, into his right eye and flew away with something in its mouth.

Orrin screaming.

The other boys stood stunned. One boy, taking a stumbling step back and tripping and falling, sprained his wrist but did not notice.

The bird had taken Orrin's right eye.

The pattern on the Androtti house wasn't Orrin and his big feet. The pattern was Orrin's right eye and the two notches carved alongside by a bird's wrathful, vengeful, fleeting perch.

For two months after the attack, Orrin never left his house except for hospital visits. The first month he had gauze and bandages, the second an eyepatch, and once a week the doctors cleaned the socket. They did not want anything migrating to the brain and polluting it further.

After two months, Orrin did the opposite of never leaving the house. He stayed on the streets, all hours, marauding and antagonizing. No eyepatch. One eye and one chapped red gully. He was a poisonous young man. Whereas before he was rude and obstreperous, now he was destructive. Evil, even. Bedford Road School got its wall-mounted cameras only years later, so no one knew who broke seven ground-floor windows. But the consensus rumor was that it had been Orrin. The Science Club after manning a fundraising table for an entire Saturday afternoon outside Key Food discovered fifty dollars missing from the till—only ten minutes after Orrin happened by, appearing to listen as the kids discussed background radiation more loudly than necessary. (The club moderator, Mr. Eggert, was sufficiently convinced of Orrin's guilt that he did not react, and even relaxed his lower face in the teacher's universal sign of tacitly admiring humor without endorsing it, and did so notwithstanding the deficits of the hypothesis from a scientific standpoint, when the kids observed they were lucky Orrin had only the one eye or they'd be out a hundred dollars instead.) Roy at Village Bookstore swore it was Orrin who'd defaced the frosted-window depiction of Santa—teetering on a library ladder and stretching past a stocking to reach for a book—by key-cutting the words "Merry" and "Kissmass," respectively, on Santa's red baggy-panted buttocks, but each time he steamed about it to another customer, Yvonne tapped his wrist a gentle reproof and said, "We don't know that," and Roy, staring off ahead of him at a private horizon, the way Roy does, retorted each time, axiomatically, irrefutably, "I know what I know."

And then there was the day that Orrin, waiting behind the library, forced Garrett Thornwood to lower his pants, crouch down in a corner, and show Orrin what it looked like when he pulled down the underwear, too. Orrin giving directions in a flat voice. It was later that day—the chronology is inarguable—that walking near his house, the Androttis' house, long abandoned by woodpeckers, not a single report of a woodpecker for months, Orrin had his other eye pecked out.

Was it the same bird? Again: I will not abet the mythmaking. It's strange enough what actually happened.

They say Orrin did more to Garrett behind the library that day. That's what the people in Pleasantville say. But they don't know. No one knows, except Garrett's family. And except the authorities—whom Garrett's family alerted that evening, when they found out. Ree Ree Godulio, who was engaged to Bobby Crenshaw when he was still with Pleasantville P.D. and had not yet moved out to Suffolk County, and who supposedly cheated on Bobby with the FBI agent who came to interview her as part of Bobby's background check after he applied (unsuccessfully) to join the Bureau, used to talk like she had inside information and went on about how Orrin tied Garrett's wrists before doing horrible things to him. As usual, Ree Ree Godulio was half right and half wrong and entirely obnoxious. What everybody knows, however, is that when Garrett came home from the library that day, his parents and certainly his brother knew something was off, because Garrett, a quiet boy, could not stop talking. He was weird. He confessed and confessed, reciting misdeeds he had perpetrated months and years earlier—Metro-North railbed collecting, clambering onto a giant red backhoe, stealing Sean Duffy's baseball mitt, returning Sean Duffy's baseball mitt by secreting it back into Sean Duffy's gym bag at soccer practice but only after it had shrunken a little from being left out in the rain the week before—but conspicuously omitting even with this new garrulousness any mention of what, if anything, had happened that day. His parents, and certainly his brother, figured out something had.

The mark on the Androttis' house: It wasn't an omega. It wasn't an *O* on feet. Birds can't read. It wasn't an eye with claw marks alongside.

It was what a woodpecker sees upon taking flight from a nearby roof and, in one swift movement, perching atop a foul boy's head and tipping forward and bowing over and plucking fast and surveying for a lightning moment, from that upside-down vantage, what justice looks like, freshly wreaked: two sightless slits where eyes should have been and a wide screaming mouth.

Today, decades later, Orrin is a different person. He is, to all appearances, a humble person, a gentle person. Those who knew him in adolescence and in his twenties have something to say about whether these incidents were what changed him, or whether it was instead the soft improvement worked by life's steady erosions. No doubt Orrin would still be telling the story, no doubt leaving out the most important part, regarding his listener earnestly, maybe needily, and pointing out the two Neapolitan scars (white center, pink border, brown frontier) alongside his right eye socket and saying, "If you look closely, you can still see where the bird landed on my face." Except that the birds robbed him even of the opportunity to extend this bonhomie, because it is superfluous. You don't need to be told where to look. The damage is easily observable to the ambling passerby.

Garrett dropped out of college and became a writer. Serious enough to file taxes under a business name. He even had a few commercial successes. The book he was proudest of was not one of them. *Gabbro and Potash Wage Infinite War*. It is, first and foremost, a vehicle for villains, unsubtly and unapologetically rendered villains, tremendous villains, each one a living breathing *casus belli* (one is actually named Cassius Belly, yes, a boxer who early in his career surrenders to gluttony), a beautiful pretext for battle scenes and modes of destruction that just sprawl. On page 166, Gabbro appears to abandon Potash in his time of need. It is a short scene, a micro-scene lasting a single paragraph, but the reader is made to understand that Potash has fallen prey to the foulest of these villains and suffers unspeakably. Of all the things Garrett wrote, it is my least favorite.

As kids we were close. Calling us close as grown men would be overstating it. Our relationship fell more in line with keeping in touch and getting together some. Garrett never came back to Pleasantville. Which was understandable. He moved down to the city, then back up and across the river to Neversink, in Sullivan County. When the parents were still around, we traveled to see him every Thanksgiving as a group. And Christmas, though not usually Christmas Day, but the weekend after, so we'd have plenty of time with him. And the two times he checked himself into Catskill Regional, the mental health unit, which of course were his lowest points.

Chronic challenges almost always mean something biochemical. There were plenty of indications this was true of Garrett, including a diagnosis or two. But the world takes its people as it finds them. And if you're a sensitive type, chances are you're absorbing what's happening to you including the toxic, especially the toxic, and if you're a quiet type, chances are you're letting it collect and intensify and germinate undisturbed.

I once tried to talk to him about it. It was after his first hospital stay, and because I didn't get it together until late in the week, we ended up spending New Year's together. Just him and me—my wife home with the newborn—watching way too many movies.

You're supposed to talk about stuff. I don't recall exactly how I asked him. But it was that New Year's that he paused and looked at his hands, and then looked up with this sweet smile and said, "I'd rather think about other things." It was a strange smile. It was a carefree smile. Strange coming with those words.

Orrin uses a cane. I'm pretty sure he uses it wrong. He stabs at the air with it, rather than sweeping and tapping from side to side. Good for keeping rodents from one's ankles, not so good for walking.

People who lose their eyes often replace them with glass facsimiles. This is, as I understand it, what people in Orrin's circumstance routinely do. But he never has. I don't know why. Perhaps they run too expensive, perhaps he feels no need. Ree Ree claims that she once asked him, and that Orrin said glass eyes were cosmetic and so an option for douche-bags, his word. But I am finished listening to Ree Ree.

Instead he wears sunglasses. Brown ones, not black, with some kind of very subtle leopard-type spotting along the arms of them. The leopard spots are apropos by one remove, because some of the kids in Pleasantville are notorious: they stalk the man like hunting cats when they encounter him, circling around him, sidling up against him, hoping to glimpse those raw gaps in his head. These are almost exclusively middle-schoolers. The elementary-school-age children are too timid and polite to try this, the high-schoolers either too indifferent or too conscientious. The middle-schoolers have little compunction and no self-restraint, and they stiffen their heads and necks (as if this will deter others from observing them) and walk tinily in a direction other than where they're looking (as if this will grant them further invisibility) until they are in line with the corner of Orrin's face and, with enough luck, a light source beyond.

I see Orrin around. Everybody does. He haunts Pleasantville. He shifts through that subset of its establishments that do not require much money to stay awhile. I see him at the library sometimes. He does not visit for the books—they have no Braille section, and in any event I once heard he never learned Braille—but to socialize with the librarians. Which, and please understand that I have a surpassing affection for libraries and librarians, is like traveling to England for the weather. The librarians do not know what to do. The ones at the Circulation Desk grasp the edge of the counter, and visibly collapse into a tighter hunch, and look at him uncertainly and follow his lead and make a nervous attempt at prattling along. The ones at the Reference Desk, intent on exuding authority, survey the room as he speaks at them and ration out replies of under five words.

For my part, when I encounter him, I fall somewhere between Circulation and Reference. I play off my interactions with him just fine—very casually, I think, very straightforwardly. Except my mouth fills with spit, and the flavor of this spit is not good, which is odd because a person as a rule does not taste his own spit. The first few times this happened, I chalked it up to nervousness. But this man does not make me nervous. That is not the right word.

Most often I see him at L&L's. L&L Deli, across the street from Michael's Tavern, gets a modest trickle of business in the Old Village. It's first choice among Pleasantvillians from whom hurry has wrested choice: eggless housewives with batter in the bowl, undercaffeinated workmen with morning shifts. No one goes to L&L's for comfort. Beyond shelves, coolers, and a register counter, it offers only a pair of saucer-on-stick tables, one chair each, smashed against the snack-item endcaps to make room for the strip of all-weather carpet that runs from the entrance along the foot of the counter like the sick rangy hide of a big-game beast put out of its lupus misery. By contrast, Jean-Jacques has all that space and all those tables, every one of them a four-top, stay as long as you like, but you'll never see Orrin at Jean-Jacques. It is, of course, more expensive than L&L's, but still plenty reasonable, and in fact a fantastic deal given the quality of the food and the painfully good French toast—but this is the difference: sitting at a table at Jean-Jacques, bereft of sight, one might not be able to tell when each customer enters or leaves. One might not feel the outdoors on his face each time someone walks in. Orrin likes to sit at L&L's, facing the door, head up and expectant, at the table farther from the door as if to suggest he is open to company but not anxious after it. Sometimes his posture suggests the opposite—a pining for every person who happens inside to stop and talk. Other times it looks like he's minding his own business, and just doing his best, and listening as acutely as possible so that he won't miss the little to which he is privy.

Months ago I stopped at L&L's on the way home for a gallon of fat-free. I saw Orrin there, at his usual table, and I said nothing. I headed straight back to the coolers, fished out a gallon of two-percent because they were out of fat-free, they always are, and went to the counter and paid. I kept my head down all the while to discourage Vincent, the owner's nephew, who gets all the early shifts and all the late shifts because he is the baby of the family, from any conversation, because if Orrin heard my voice he'd know it was me, he'd know I'd decided not to acknowledge him. I left without saying a word.

I kept my head down even between the counter and the door, even though the transaction was done and Vincent could no longer entangle me in talk. Why? Some childish presentiment that Orrin could somehow see me with those chafed orbits of his? A kind of embarrassment that I was being so ugly, that I was effectively lying to a disabled man?

No. Head down is the easiest position for setting the jaw with conviction against doing what one badly wants to do.

I think Orrin knew it was me. Ever since that day, he's strange with me. Now when he talks to me, he presents more guarded, as if hedging his bets against everything in general, and he pauses each time it's his turn to say something, weighing what he knows about me, considering things. This may be my imagination. But I don't think so.

And every time Orrin sees me, without fail—it was this way before the two-percent milk pickup, it has been this way after—he asks how Garrett is. And like every other person in Pleasantville, I lie to him. I say my brother's fine. I say Garrett's doing the usual, working hard. Because Orrin still does not know about Garrett. We've kept this knowledge from Orrin. Everybody in Pleasantville. There was no meeting at which this was decided. No flyers were handed out, no notice posted just inside the west door of Key Food. Just came to be that no one told him about Garrett's passing, and no one's going to tell him.

You might suppose this is an act of generosity. Like the reassurance of a smile that looks carefree but can't possibly be. I don't know about everybody else. For everybody else, maybe it is. It's certainly an act of inadvertent brutality, though. Because I speculate that all Orrin has left is his conversations with people. And I keep mine short so that I don't have to lie more than necessary. I know other people do the same—I overhear their conversations with Orrin at the Farmer's Market, where he positions himself equidistant from the ice-pop stand and the falafel booth, like the Statue of Liberty in New York Harbor, where people debouching at that end of the market onto Manville Road have to pass him and so see him and so talk to him. They keep their interactions short, because they're fundamentally good people, and though I imagine the subject of Garrett rarely comes up in their conversations with Orrin—he was my brother, not theirs, no reason why he should come up—they know this has been kept from him, they feel themselves guilty by this knowledge alone, and so they avoid extended interactions with Orrin.

For me it isn't an act of generosity. I've fantasized a thousand times about sitting down at that ridiculous mini-table at L&L's.

This is how it goes:

"How are you, Orrin."

"Kevin? How's it going, Kevin?"

I wait.

"Well," I say, "I suppose I like myself."

I wait some more.

"Yeah," I say. "I guess that's how I'd put it. I guess I like myself."

"What?" he says.

And this is when I reach over and take those absurd sunglasses off his face and stare into the blank flaps in his head. These are, of course, the ultimate in elsewhere eyes. Eyes do not get deader. I wager if he had them back in his head, they'd be no livelier, because to put on clothes in the morning and to talk to people about the river-wide aisles at the new Walgreens and to take breaths and expel breaths like a normal person, this perpetrator of cruelty must always be averting himself from—in fact denying—the central event of his life.

This one doesn't deserve pity. The prosecutors, they pitied him. Blind, juvenile, disfigured. Son of a county commissioner. Do not pity him.

"My brother is dead," is how I answer. "He had problems all his life because of you. He killed himself because of you. He died from what you did to him."

I don't know if that's true. Garrett didn't leave a note. You'd think a writer of all people might find the wherewithal. You'd think a brother of all people might take a minute.

Here's another thing: I don't know that it matters. Orrin deserves to think it is. He deserves at least to wonder.

I get up and leave. Likely it's Saturday, because on weekdays I work in the city and don't get the opportunity to visit L&L's. So I go home and have myself a nice Saturday evening dinner with my wife and my son, perhaps watch some television, go to bed. The next day I pretend to do other things. It's pretending because it's a show of industry to distract me from the only thing that matters. Because on Sunday, after waiting until what I find myself suspecting is a reasonable time, and then putting that suspicion out of my head and setting my attention instead to emptying the basement dehumidifier and bringing up an extra two rolls of paper towels and collecting the recyclables that overnight have blown out of the bin into Gary's yard, and then in early afternoon letting myself think yet a second time and therefore with unimpeachable reason that I have waited long enough, I get in the car, park it in the public lot behind where A'Mangiare used to be, cross the street, and turn right at the Sunoco. And I walk into L&L's. I open the door and walk right in.

And one of two things is true. Possibly, but not probably, indeed more like merely conceivably, that man is nowhere to be found, because he went home the night before and, properly disabused, finally shamed, got a belt or a gun and did himself in. Or, more likely, that man is sitting there as usual, facing the door, waiting for me to plunge the knife I have brought with me straight into one of those sockets and finish what the peckers started and continue until I feel the blade knock knock knock against the back of his skull, knock once, twice, three times—each knock a different sound, progressively hollower for what I imagine, perhaps fancifully but I don't care, is the liquefaction of those contents that initially gave it a solid, gavel-like timbre—against the back of that filthy skull.

This is why I keep silent. This is why I don't tell Orrin Androtti what he's done. Sometimes silence feels like cowardice. Sometimes I feel like I owe it to my brother to do otherwise. But I would kill him—I would—and rage is the reason, fucking rage, and maybe it *is* cowardice that I don't destroy that which Pleasantville spends so much of its time tiptoeing around. I'm not proud of any of it, none of it feels good, nothing born of horribleness can get good. But it's at least a reason, and at least I know the reason, and so when Garrett appears to me in my dreams—never as a full-grown man, always a boy—that reason is one thing we don't need to talk about because he knows already.

Pleasantville still gets woodpeckers every fall. As for Rich McCabe, he's still around. He's ancient now. You can ask him about hooded falcons. You can even just mention falcons, any sort of falcons, within his earshot. I know because I get a drink now and then with Paul Shires, and Shires, stranded in suburbia and eager to make his own excitement, has tried it. The way Shires tells it, Rich, he'll shake his head, but only after bowing it first, so that the top of his skull moves like an undecided drill bit. And he'll mutter "Hell." His voice is a rasp now. And he'll leave it at that. And because the old man can't be made to say more, Shires says it's even chances whether he's thinking of the latest birds and venting frustration, or instead thinking of those strange days one strange autumn and naming the responsible party.

THE DUPLEX AND
THE SCARP

The duplex experience is an outsized thing.

Its double current cooks the flesh off the commonplace. Its monarch girth—this and that, too—cows the imagination.

"Don't come upstairs yet," she says.

"Why not?" he says.

Sex is a duplex.

It had better be. The species depends on it. This one-two cannot disappoint: the sweet thrill of cumming, the heady and barbarous intimacy that precedes.

"I'm still changing."

"I've seen you change a thousand times."

The Siberian gulag: a fine illustration of the duplex. The ultimate prison within a prison. Win escape and, congratulations, win freezing unsurvivable desolation.

Its doubleness famously crushed hope like no other scheme ever devised. Remember the Dachau survivor who, told he was being transferred to Kolyma, promptly hanged himself.

"How was work?"

"Terrible. Work was terrible. Also the way you just tried to change the subject. That was terrible. I'm coming upstairs."

The death of a loved one is the ultimate duplex experience. Lose the person and lose also a swath of your own life. The years shared, the memories nurtured.

Whole decades are bled of meaning without the someone to remember them with. Or force-injected with a septic resin—one part despair (what could be the worth of something so contingent to begin with?) and one part despair (what I had I will never have again . . .)—until they blacken and fall away.

"We should talk about it first."

"I'm just coming upstairs. Not even the bedroom. I'll just stay in the hallway. I like to be on the same floor as my wife when I talk to her. Crazy that way."

If your loved one dies (or leaves, but—for clarity's sake—let's assume here that every end is a death, which is to say, let's assume the truth), you may recover. You may "get over it," meaning paralysis turns merely to sadness like a harness. You may one day regain a life the pointlessness of which is not its most salient quality. This is not a sure thing. This depends, goes the conventional wisdom, on a welter of factors: the felt profundity of your relationship with the departed; the variety and poignance of other items in your life with perceived existential significance; your unparticular adaptability; your penchant for nostalgia. Whether you're the sort for whom tears salt the wound or salve it, because there will be plenty.

Or you may not.

He comes upstairs. He does not stay in the hallway. He moves to the bedroom door and pushes it partway open. He watches her. It is the first time he has seen her naked, except bandaging, since the surgery.

She turns and sees him and screams.

Let's put aside the embroidery. Let's get to the truth of it. There is no welter of factors. There is one factor. Time. It is time that decides whether you survive the death that matters. Specifically: Take the years you spent with your loved one. No. Take the years you lived in love with your loved one. Take the years, months, days you spent learning how the smell of the back of her neck reacted chestnuttily to sunshine. Add these. Be meticulous. Because it will take you equally long after the loss, precisely the same amount of time after she dies, until you breathe again and notice the sky and let yourself do something so small as worry.

Nick meets Seth on October 1, falls in love on November 1, and loses him forever in a funicular accident on December 1. (Nick watches from below—a fear of heights pairs well with a cup of concession hot chocolate—as the machine jolts to a stop, then gives a shiver, then drops decisively from the line overhead like an untreed apple. There is a reeling minute when, notwithstanding his yelps, and his forearms vising the sides of his head, the Brazilian tourists milling nearby believe Nick's alarm general and do not guess he is watching his boyfriend die.) Until December 30, Nick will be lost. On December 30, Nick will blink and look around and, though hurting yet, realize the mist was of his own making.

A real racket is what she puts up. Protests, a profanity. A con-
flagration of the face.

He walks steadily, inert to her noise. He moves with his hands
folded behind his back, park-stroll-style. It is a weird mode of prog-
ress that can mean No Big Deal, and Couldn't Hurt You if I Tried,
and All the Time in the World. He does not stop until nearly he col-
lides with her body, this new body that she holds concavely, that she
keeps in a posture of begging pardon. He staggers down to his knees.
His hands still behind his back, he kisses her stomach. He kisses her
hipbones and their sidecar notches. He is careful about his head. He
kisses her thighs, between them. He will not let his head graze the
bandaging.

The corollary: There is always a midway point. There is
always a point exactly halfway between the moment you fall
in love and the moment you die. This fulcrum, this pivot,
determines survivability. If the two of you make it past that
point alive and together, then that's the good news. The bad
news: If the two of you make it past that point, and your
loved one predeceases you, you'll never recover. There is simply not enough time. This pivot, in short, is a cliff.

Will meets Eve, a friend of an invitee who abhors a train
ride into the city alone, at his thirtieth birthday party. Their
love is near instant. (His: when at the restaurant she abruptly
sits at the table and plants an elbow onto a fork and the
pain bodies forth as a mutter, "Fuck me." Hers: when, hearing this, he shakes his head smiling and horse-soothes, "Too
soon.") On Will's sixtieth birthday, he will choke on his cake
and die. Actually, it will appear so to those present—ardent
eyes, purpling face—but in fact it is a massive stroke he will
suffer, the cake in his mouth of no comfort and indeed a

positive terror to his guests for it will batter up his drool into a froth. His last thought might have been lacerating (serves me right for wishing selfish in a room full of grandchildren) but is instead another smiling shake of the head (of course I had to wish for health). Eve, a widow at fifty-eight, dies at eighty-seven. One year short of heart's reprieve.

She takes his head and brings it against her.

His ear presses against her navel. If his own breathing is an ocean, then he hears the ocean. He does not hear hers. But he feels it. Her trunk is fitful against his face. He breathes in time with its ragged swells and capitulations. This is how crying becomes a sound like laughter.

Just like that, in the space of an afternoon, by a happenstance of the calendar, one of them has pivoted. One of them without knowing has lived the point of no return, leapt off the scarp, innocent of how she has condemned herself this day.

I will not tell you who will die first. I will not pretend it is this fact that matters most. But here is what I will tell you: Just like that, in the space of an afternoon, by a happenstance of the calendar, one of them has pivoted. One of them without knowing has lived the point of no return, leapt off the scarp, innocent of how he has sanctified himself this day.

JOHN TAN CAN'T PLAY CLASSICAL GUITAR

I WAS TEN WHEN I TOOK UP CLASSICAL GUITAR WITH A DWARF.

He wore thick glasses. The ends of his mustache dipped frownishly around his mouth. He spoke like a squeaky puppet.

I do not recall how he came to be my instructor. There is an age—the year varies but not the phenomenon—prior to which life is largely inflicted and grossly inexplicable. Likely my mother, the maker in our household of the happening of things, was responsible. Maybe she spotted his name in what passed in our Florida town for a newspaper article. Maybe she found a magic conch that whispered a warm but measured endorsement.

He was disabled. He staggered from the hip and used a crutch with a forearm cuff. I had no idea how old he was. He was the first dwarf I'd ever met. The striking novelty of him deterred speculation.

The lessons were at his apartment. Except for the dog, he lived alone. I never saw anyone else in his apartment. I never saw him talk on the phone. I never heard him speak anyone's name, including my own.

He had one outfit. White shirt, black pants, black shoes. Only later in life would I recognize it. It was the uniform of the conspicuously serious of purpose: ring bearers, caterers, valet parkers, trattoria waiters, junior Mormons, junior prommers, undertakers. Once he wore a denim jacket. This was a solitary episode of hipness that made me unaccountably glad and never occurred again.

The dog was a little nervous one with sad peanut eyes and a crumb of a penis. He spent his time stippling the apartment's carpet with tiny cairns of pebbly waste. I never saw him make one of these. But their number, their sheer coverage, suggested a campaign. They made a massive checkerboard, every piece kinged two, three times. The apartment reeked. Oddly, though, of urine, not feces—which seemed just another emasculation. He was a dog hung with a peppercorn, his owner could not walk him, and even his doody was impotent to give a proper stink.

After one lesson I felt very, very sad for this dog. After three I wondered if this was an expedient pity, if I had pushed it one species away to make it bearable.

My father drove me. The apartment building resembled a motel, might have been previously. It had no elevator, and the unit was on the second floor. Strange for someone with a crutch. Nor were there interior hallways. The apartment was at the end of a breezeway. This should, and normally would, have been a bit of magic. I was the child of immigrants. Rarely did we go on trips, and when we did, we slept in motels. In my tender head, therefore, breezeways were long pieces of vacation. They were lucky implausibilities: open like hedge mazes, but you got to walk on the wall; open like convertibles, but always parked and waiting.

This particular breezeway, however, was different. It was a gangplank slick with dread. I never practiced for these lessons. And the grim ritual of it, the procession each week to a distant door for which I was unprepared, was only made worse by its matter-of-factness. Each straightforward step was a taste of the shaming impassivity that awaited me on the other side, because the man there similarly would not make a big deal, would not protest, would not reveal the slightest annoyance, but rather would simply comment, dutifully and without reproof, on what (a lot) needed work for next time. This breezeway warned me that I was about to be found out.

Always the door was ajar. Always my father knocked on it anyway. "Come in," we heard from one of the bedrooms. My father went first. He held the door open as the guitar and I tried bad angles. Then he scooted around to lead through that turd-garden. As he did so he resembled a dystopian robot, my father, a robot equipped with a crap-detector. He walked rigidly as—with a rigid arm, in rigid silence—he pointed out the closest nuggets so that I might avoid them.

The lights were never on. I wondered about sensitive eyes. (No, I told myself. That's albinos.) I wondered whether the man was poor and trying to save on electricity. (Bigot. Why not assume he leaves the door open to trap rats for mealtime?) Picking my way through that dimness, it occurred to me, more than once, that visitors denied scat-free passage

might at least be afforded the one help—a little illumination—
that was readily available. (The nerve of him. When there was
so much more he could do, like drape a silk handkerchief over
his crutch-cuff and personally escort you through the dark.
Or just put you on his shoulders and carry you like a burro.)

The dog, shy, made only fleeting appearances while tran-
siting rooms.

At last, the spare bedroom. It was the studio, empty but
for two chairs, a music stand, a functioning bulb overhead.
At the center of this wan affair sat my teacher. He did not get
up when we came. Nor did he pretend—as he might have, as
people so often do—that he was busy with something else,
something lofty and engrossing. One of us was honest with
the other.

Somehow the dog knew to respect this room. The carpet
here was fouled, no doubt, but less densely than in the other
rooms. This small relativity was special. It made no sense, but
the space between piles bespoke luxury.

After several lessons, I questioned if the dread I always
felt plodding that breezeway owed at all to my not having
practiced. I wondered if the feeling was in fact the ache of a
conscience depleted. Soreness meant muscle fatigue, dizzi-
ness a shortfall in some essential like oxygen or nourishment.
Maybe the dread of that breezeway approach came of trying not to think about him waiting, trying not to conjecture
how long before we arrived he must have arranged himself so
that we would find him seated. Maybe it came of pretending,
week upon week, not to feel sorry for a grown man.

I took the empty chair. My father, having entered the studio first, simply nodded, then withdrew into the living room.

I don't know how or where he waited, sitting or standing. Nor do I remember my father and my teacher ever talking. If they did, I can't imagine how it would have gone. My father knew about money and hard people and selling muffins at the coffee counter in a hospital lobby and the impact on profits of a miniature POW-MIA flag next to a tip cup and making his ten-year-old assistant manager pick at the start of each day during his summer break which fifteen minutes would be the only fifteen minutes during which he'd be allowed to sit. In his mind, all art was frivolous, and all artists drug addicts. He agreed to music lessons because he had an inkling about résumés and college applications and, perhaps relatedly, because my mother was the maker in our household of the happening of things.

But that afternoon my rigid, grudging father knocked, and there came no answer, and my father knocked again, and still nothing, and, looking at the foot of the door, he opened it away from him. I followed inside. As he called out and we waited, I thought about how if I were a mathematical genius like that fourth-grader John Tan, I might figure out the one place where I could set down the guitar on the carpet without disturbing a single star in that wrong constellation. But I was no genius, and such a place did not present itself, and my father was already moving forward. Again I followed, but now he was coming out of the studio and walking toward the kitchen and saying, Stay there, Stephen, stay there. He never called me Stephen. He moved into the kitchen and out of sight. I thought I'd misunderstood. It was lesson time, my guitar wasn't getting lighter. I walked to the spare bedroom.

Lying there on the carpet was the dwarf. He rested exactly on his back. His glasses had fallen alongside his face. His mouth was open but not a lot, which gave him a look of alertness, as if he were deciding what to say. There was an odor. A different one. A hiked pant leg showed a bare calf, like a yeasty dinner roll, but with hair, more hair than on my father's leg. I was puzzling over the virility of that hair, in this compromised person, when I saw that on that same calf was a spot. Like a bruise. I backed up a step. Strangely, it was the spot that threatened, more than the dead body itself. I looked closer and saw that the spot was raised, a welt of some kind. Had someone beaten him? No, a single mark meant nothing. I heard my father's voice. He was on the phone. He was using the very slow voice he saved for Americans who were having trouble understanding him, and the slow way he had of talking made it singsongy, and this singsonginess in most voices suggested the kind of condescension that starts fights. But my father, who toyed with people and told them northern Spain and southern Romania and everywhere except where he really was from, got away with it because the exotic gets the benefit of the doubt, and the rough gets wide berth, and so he got both.

And then I noticed the dog. He was facing the opposite wall. I don't know why or how I hadn't noticed him before. He was squatting every few seconds. Every few seconds he was crouching over his owner, but nothing happened. And then he'd take a nervous walk around, looking at the floor in front of him, never at the dwarf—or at me—and then he'd try again, his tiny haunches quivering in the air over some part of the man, his ankle, his arm, his belly. The spot was the dog's. Likely he'd left it some time ago, because now nothing was happening. At one point the dog, his eyes sad as always, hovered over the dwarf's face. He did not look at him, even then. And he did not pause, as he turned this way and that, as his nose made quirky assessing movements. He was sure he had his work cut out for him.

Days later my mother learned it had been a stroke. But we knew nothing as we waited on the breezeway. I don't remember turning my back on the body, or leaving the dog. But I remember that the spot was only the first indecency of that afternoon. For after the police and paramedics came, I heard through the door, ajar as before, the word "fuck" two times and "shit" many more, spoken by several voices, and laughter. I remember looking up at my father as we waited, as I leaned against the breezeway railing, he with one hand on a hip and the other ready at his side, and it occurred to me that he never leaned. The way he was standing, the sun shone through the wing of his nostril and made the ball of it a bright glowing orange, and then he'd move just a touch and the color would dim to chickeny yellow, and he'd move back and his nose would catch fire again. I understood even then that the dog had not been burying his owner. The world was not Disney, though I hadn't been. Nor had the dog mistaken the dwarf for carpet. Life was not dumb cruelty, though my parents warned me plenty. The dog was simply trying to get on without his friend, and failing, and, not knowing what else to do, marking the territory of loss. I understood with a pulse of resentment that an immigrant father is very much the opposite of a movie father, who might propose first with a sly grin and then a broad smile that perhaps there was a little incontinent orphan of a dog in need of adopting. But I also understood that my father was a maker, when it counted, of the making sense of things, this man who—and I saw it, for otherwise I would not have believed it—refused to charge for coffee the ones who looked like they'd been crying. And when we left and stopped on the way home at the cut-rate supermarket and picked up plums and milk and an economy-size box of unsweetened puffed wheat, and put them in plastic bags that we'd use to line the waste baskets and to ferry books on Saturday trips to the public library and to pack bathroom items for our triennial vacations, I was grateful for all of it, and for a father who called me son.

ABRIDGED

It had flowed brilliantly once.

No longer. His nouns squatted there, like deserted artillery. His verbs lifted nothing. They just bent the sentences in half. The remaining parts of speech sagged one way or the other.

He noticed something else: His typing hands felt as cumbersome as the lumps of prose they left behind.

"The flight was long and crowded and exhausting. She still felt like throwing everything up and couldn't get to sleep. He felt a bit feverish himself. He drank too much rum and ginger ale, replacing one wooze with another. He knew the restrooms when they were pristine and when his fellows had abandoned all decency.

Life was not perfect, but three things were supposed to be: A couple's first sex. Their wedding. And the honeymoon.

The wedding's perfection he had had little to do with. There were too many people involved, too many other expectations dictating every parameter. The blur and volume of events gave the illusion they moved under their own power. It was a trick of cold fusion: compress enough bodies into a time and space and they seem to generate their own fate. The process even had its effluents. His best man had failed to return the tuxedoes on time. Also the marriage was thirty-six hours old and still unconsummated.

The honeymoon, on the other hand: Its perfection was his responsibility. If it failed, he failed. All else equal, this counseled in favor of initiative, vigor, zeal. Things left alone did not a memory make. This is the first and great commandment, he thought, and the second is like unto it. Presented with a choice between action and inaction, between doing and passivity, he must do. For the next several days, he must always do.

When he saw a passenger across the aisle struggling with a can of pomegranate juice, he reached out a hand.

'Mind if I give it a try?'

'Sure, thank you,' she said, surrendering it.

The tab had fused with the top of the can. Probably old inventory. He looked at the expiration date: next year. Perhaps an unheated warehouse, or a damp one. His left thumbnail worked stubbornly beneath the tab. It was longer than his other nails—an optimal length that did not get in the way of things, but could smooth into and under and between them. He used the tip of his index finger for counterweight to prevent the can from tipping. The single fingertip was stagecraft. The juice answered with its own flourish: a congratulatory sfitz on opening, though it wasn't carbonated.

His wife was turned the other way. She was asleep finally. He knew this because no one said, 'Show off much?'

'That's handy,' the woman said as she took back the can. 'A sort of utility thumbnail. Is that an American thing?' She was slightly older than him, and slightly better looking.

'This guy?' He looked down at the nail and wiped at it with the other thumb. It always felt wrong to use the ordinary thumb to groom the strong one. Like forcing Cain to wash Abel. But he never remembered this rule until immediately after breaking it.

'No,' he said. 'It's a third-grade thing. I was undefeated in arm-wrestling. No rule about what you do with your thumb.'

She laughed.

'And I was right-handed,' he added. 'So they should have been suspicious when I'd only go lefties.'

She laughed more.

'You're not American?' he asked.

'Canadian,' she said.

'Oh, Canada.' Immediately he realized these were the first two words of the national anthem. But he did not wish to appear glib or disrespectful and so left it alone. Instead he held up his thumb between them like a candle. 'If it were up to me, I think I'd put this under our border. I'd pry it off, and flip it north. To the Arctic. So we can be one country already.'

She did not like this. She did not like it at all. She pursed her lips and said, 'Well,' and poured out some of the juice into a cup and returned to her reading.

An hour later, his head squashed into the gap between seats, he achieved a long doze. He thought of L. He tried not to. First time he saw her was at a reading. First thing he told her was a lie. 'No, it's not taken.' His friend had to find somewhere else to sit. She had a wound of a mouth. His eyes liked to lick it when she talked. For years he burned to see her in an emergency. Now where's that gentleness? he'd ask. He tried not to wonder what L. would think of his wife. His wife was a practical person. She liked to stay where she excelled: on the surface of the everyday. It respected the sharp and adept and peremptory in her. That busy panache, that assuredness, had attracted him in the first place. But this was no good to anybody. This was unhealthy, immature, having both of them in mind at the same time. He needed to stop. Would the two of them have been friends in another life? Could they see something in each other to admire? His first weeks with L., he experienced a brittle wonder at whether her kind of earnestness was really possible. The sensation lessened over time. He'd hoped it was a growing pain, dwindling as he became better himself. In the end, what he became was more prolific. Because the last thing he ever said to her was two lies. 'You have to. I can't lose you.' Yes, apparently, he could. And she didn't have to forgive anyone.

By the time they landed, his wife felt worse.

'You'll take a nice hot shower,' he told her, 'and you'll rest up a bit, and you'll feel molto betterissimo. I promise.'

'That's sweet. I hope you tell the future better than you talk Italian.'

'Four years of it in high school.'

'I thought you took Spanish.' She was squinting. Now the cabin light seemed carbonated.

'Habla one romance language, you hablar them all. Which reminds me.' He bent to excavate a shoulder bag from under the seat and emerged red-faced. 'Soon as you feel better, the only language you'll hear from me will be the language of love.'

'God. Give me one of those little bags from the seatback pocket.' She squeezed his hand.

They waited for the plane doors to open. The delay was long enough, the cabin warm enough, that an exotic climate soon prevailed and castes emerged: the aisled nobility, standing tall and placid; the stoopbacked peasantry, upper bodies crammed against the overheads, restive and flashing jealous eyes; the clergy, cool to impulse and stewarding the blessings of seated comfort. He took the opportunity to squinch a half-turn under the overhead until he faced the Canadian passenger.

'I'm sorry about what I said. About Canada. I didn't mean anything.'

She glanced at him only briefly from her seat and said, 'Good, good.' She spoke this without antipathy, as if thinking about something more pressing.

When they got off the plane, his wife still looked weak. He urged her to take it slow. But she felt hurried. The roped-off passageway to Customs was narrow, which made it difficult for other passengers to pass. She was self-conscious about holding people up.

'Don't worry about it. People want to pass, they'll pass.'

Plus, he persuaded her, the veteran air traveler knew better than to enter a Customs line too early. Front of the line meant the Customs officers were still sharp to ask questions.

Back of the line meant a smaller mass of waiting travelers and so less implicit pressure on the same officers to keep the questions brief. Safety lived in the middle ranks. Theirs had been among the first rows to deplane. So they were better off lagging.

'I love you, baby, but you are full of crap.' She wiped her forehead with her sleeve. 'What you need to declare at Customs is a load of crap.'

An American family, voices like party favors, stood in line under a giant placard reading EU PASSPORTS ONLY. He was about to point this out to his wife when he noticed the family's patriarch leave the group to pick up a piece of paper on the floor a few feet away. The man examined the item—plainly an airline boarding pass stub. He looked up, held out his new find meaningfully, and shouted, over and over, with the stern authority of someone entrusted with life-and-death business, revolving slowly so no ear could miss a precious syllable, 'MARCO POLO? MARCO POLO? ANYONE NAMED MARCO LOSE A TICKET? MARCO POLO?'

Was this man joking? The actual non-EU line was moving forward, and so he had to leave this scene, but he persisted long enough to learn—from the way the man's family huddled self-consciously, tucked their chins as they took turns explaining that Marco Polo was the airport's name and so appeared on every boarding pass (this should have not required more than one of them), looked on with low-lidded grins of embarrassed condescension as he examined his own boarding pass for verification—that, no, indeed, he had not been joking.

Was he joking about not having been joking?

The line moved, and then didn't. It was the usual bous-trophedon. A sham of progress where there was only a loop, pointless and endless and involuted. Along this herd path he saw the same people again and again. He stared through a glaze, allotting equal time to these and to daydreams. A woman ahead of them was wearing the very same shoes as his wife—Mary Janes, except his wife's were slate gray and this woman's were custard yellow. The slate was easily the more tasteful. A man behind them held a toddler in a crooked arm; they took turns, father pretending to bite off daughter's nose, daughter slapping father across the face, hard.

His first sex ever was with Janet Pelkin. The stupendous heat and wet of her vagina were too good to be true. Two moments after he entered her—one moment too late because, regrettably, one moment was all Janet needed to realize what had happened and pronounce a hauntingly ambiguous 'Wow'—he realized to his embarrassed agony he was enjoying the feel of his own semen.

The Customs officer wore epaulets and a smirk. Janet Pelkin had not worn epaulets."

Keep at it, baby, his wife said. *Even good writers have bad days.*

You mean even bad writers have good days.

Screw you, she said.

No, I didn't mean that you thought—He didn't finish. Repairs don't help a fire.

He kept at it. He wasted four years. He wasted a fifth dreaming of a market for opening paragraphs.

One night he'd had enough. And a bottle of whiskey.

The combination opened his eyes. He cut off his thumbs. Peroxide, Japanese kitchen knife, towel. The second thumb was tough for the lack of the first. The first was tough because he was drunk at three in the morning. He should not have used a white towel.

What his beautiful and unyielding wife said: *You what.* What he surmised in an exhilarated haze: she'd had enough too, finally, and this was keeping her questions from sounding like questions. What his unyielding and beautiful wife said next, and last: *You did what.*

Without stumpy counterweights, his fingers flew. Without a good way to the space bar, they worked hotly and continuously, like eight thin glands. He abandoned calculation for whim. He abandoned caution for abandonment. No longer did he dispense narrative in doted-over increments, like a cross-eyed druggist with arthritis and a distaste for children. He fairly secreted it.

This lymph was light and lovely, and sweet.

"It was late morning, but the sunlight was strangely young, almost white, when they reached the hotel. The doors to the lobby stood open. Outside a woman dressed categorically in purple walked a dog. She came to a halt in front of them. He found himself scanning her person for the cause of her trouble. She crouched a little, and put her head out in a conspiratorial jut, and so did not simply speak in a mild accent but imparted, 'The two of you look like the movie stars. Just like the movie stars.' She nodded her head and, apparently expecting no answer, yanked at the dog and moved on.

They could not afford this hotel. This fact went far to make the trip a honeymoon. Inside, the scent was immediate, as if the press of his leather sole had caressed it out of the marble threshold: luxury, satisfaction, contentment, ease. But more, a sense that all things tended in their favor. What looked like a tour group, clutched around a short round Italian man—Sicilian, maybe—moved out of the lobby soon after he and his wife entered, as if to make room. The front-desk clerk, a man of about twenty-five years and equivocal feelings about hairbrushing, greeted them with a lean over the counter.

The room key was startling. It had its own head and body and tail: an intricate brasswork, a dowel of alderwood, a gash-red tassel. It was a key that made it impossible to conceive of opening a door with a plastic card. That's the kind of key, he thought as the clerk presented it ceremoniously, that you cannot lose.

'This key you cannot lose,' said the clerk, unsmiling. Thinking it was one thing. Receiving it as instruction made him resentful. The words suggested a supreme and humorless confidence. They were the kind spoken by those who knew, without believing because belief was for the timid, that the world started where they stood.

He and his wife turned away from the counter for the elevators. He remembered he'd meant to ask about the boat tour and turned sharply around. He caught the clerk staring at his wife's ass. The clerk's head was level, only his eyes were cast downward, which meant one of two things: Either it was a furtive survey, one that did not involve the head because there was no calculation, only compulsion and helplessness and a bit of embarrassment, and arguably decency, too, for having been kept to a discreet minimum. Or it was an arrogant leer, a look that did not bother involving the head because it was half-entitled and half-dismissive and wholly presumptuous.

Every sullen fiber of him wished to believe the latter. He was tired, sore, a little sick, a little drunk. But he knew this, and wrenched himself like the dog of a purple woman into choosing the former instead.

'The hotel has its own vaporetto? The finest in town, I hear?' He smiled at the clerk.

'Vaporetto, no,' said the clerk, his eyes bland, guiltless, 'but a motor yacht, we have it, of course, sir.'

'And there's a daily tour?'

'Yes, for the guests only.'

'Leaves here when?'

'Twelve o'clock noon. From that door.' He pointed at a small door in the corner of the lobby, near an enormous vase of flowers and a seating area. The stems of the flowers were nearly as long as the brocade sofa alongside. Stalk and silk formed a delicate but incongruent L, a ballerina and her fat immaculate patron.

'Twelve o'clock? That's in an hour.'

'Indeed, sir.'

'Should I wear comfortable clothes?' He winked. 'Will I have to row?' He was not the winking sort.

The clerk did not note the humor. He nodded once. 'Yes, comfortable always is good.'

One elevator stood waiting with its doors open. The other had a piece of masking tape across its closed doors, and hanging from it a hand-lettered sign on printer paper turned landscape:

FUORI SERVIZIO
OUT OF OUDER

From behind the closed doors came a noise. More than once. Like a girl singing a wandering melody that turned a rusted corner and became a grating complaint, brief and shrill.

They took the working elevator. Their floor had a muffled quiet to it—intense, not desolate. These blank doors nurtured slow intrigues on one side to offset the bustle along the other. At the end of the corridor was their room and the promise of a coffeemaker. The lock turned with a pompous thunk. The inside of the room smelled like velvet.

They poured their suitcases and shoulder bags onto the floor. There were two queen-size beds. He sat on the one farther from the door and gave the mattress a beckoning pat, not so close alongside him that it was openly lascivious. Given she was still feeling poorly, he could not act the brute. Given it was their honeymoon, he would not act the cliché. He patted in the least horndog way he knew how.

She kicked off her shoes and, in one motion, hopped up and curled into a self-dandling *S*.

'Hot in here?' she sighed.

'I'll open a window.'

'That'll make it hotter. Check the thermostat.'

He spent a minute storking around the room. 'There is no thermostat.'

'Mm.' She burrowed into the pillow. Her hair was cozy around her face. 'Better already.'

'We gotta go,' he said. 'We gotta get going.'

'Just close my eyes.'

That is what she'd said on their wedding night. In a plainer, dollar-denominated hotel room, after getting in late from the reception. Immediately before passing out on him at three in the morning.

'Baby, we gotta go. We gotta take showers. Boat leaves in sixty minutes.' He glanced at his watch. 'Fifty minutes.'

'Go ahead and take your shower. I'll go second.'

When finally they exited the room, they did so feeling fresh and wreathed in notes of vetiver. They rode the elevator down in a cloud of vetiver with four strangers, one of them an Englishman with a finger in his nose. When they reached the lobby, they emerged into air asouse with vetiver. This was the fragrance he had noted when they first entered the hotel. He realized now it wasn't the magic he'd let himself believe. Just a critical yardage of tourist epidermis recently scrubbed with scented glycerin and passed at volume through finite space. The dumb homogenizing prettiness of hotel soap.

They reached the lobby at 11:50. He headed to the door.

'Let me run to the restroom real quick,' she said, veering off already to the opposite corner of the lobby.

'You were just in the restroom,' he called after her.

'It always doesn't,' is what he thought he heard through her trailing hair."

Time passed. His typing accelerated. His fingers whirred so fast that individual keystrokes were unobservable. His hands were two floating ballclouds of buzz, a pair of four-winged hummingbirds livid with mating urge but too delirious to come together.

His writing, once so free and fluid, careened out of control. It turned random, unaccountable, incoherent.

He wondered if this was his fault, something wrong in the execution. Or if it was inevitable and could not be helped.

He also wondered this aloud on his ex-wife's voice mail, four times, about the two of them. The last one he left at three in the morning. That particular hour was not kind to him.

He never heard back.

That was all right. He didn't even love her still.

"The clerk piped up from the front desk. 'You go on the—' The clerk did not finish and instead pointed at the same door he'd indicated an hour earlier, the boat-tour door. It occurred to him he hadn't yet looked out that door, did not know what was on the other side. Could be three monkeys playing languidly with a flashlight. Could be a lobby nearly identical to this one, where an equally overbearing version of this clerk pointed in mirror simultaneity, but where he himself did not, as he did now, feel increasingly unsteady.

'Yes,' he replied.

The clerk spoke to a man wearing a dark windbreaker and a pageboy cap. They both looked at him and then down at the floor between them as they continued talking.

He looked at his watch. It was 11:57. She was still in the restroom. A disgruntled part of him, urged to the fore by the bumps and burdens of travel and by rising nausea, speculated it would always be like this. His wife would always go to the restroom at the last minute just before they had to board or disembark or report in or check out or congregate. His life would be a series of these cliff-hanging waits or, more precisely, what transpired between them.

The inference was eminently reasonable. The prediction, however, was wrong.

Into the lobby came a group, quietly—only shoefall and the rustle of several bags. It was the same tour group as had left the lobby that morning. The Sicilian, waiting for laggards to join, stretched his stout little neck, front and sides virile with a grattato of morning growth, and peered over his own chin to take inventory. Only after they stilled in a circle around him did he pull out what looked to be a laminated map.

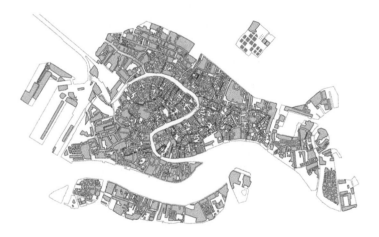

'I have spoken of the rising seas. I have spoken of the fighting which Venice makes to stay above them. I have spoken of how Venice looses this fight.'

The Sicilian roved his eyes in a deliberate circle, mule-drawn, across the chests of his charges. Their faces threatened to tantalize him off-script and were best avoided.

'It is no wonder that Venice is dying and fated to die. Look and perceive. Its very map is a picture of two fishes devouring each other. One fish swims from the west and bites the lower lip of the other. It attacks with its higher teeth, San Polo, and its lower teeth, Dorsoduro; Santa Croce is the spine.' He indicated these areas on the map without looking. 'The second fish, from the east, tries with might to swallow the first fish's head. The jaws are San Marco and Cannaregio, this powerful tail is Castello.'

The fellow in the dark windbreaker blew back into the lobby through the door, animated. He had not realized this fellow had left the lobby. Time now 11:59. Wife still in restroom.

Windbreaker stalked directly up to him. 'Sir, it has to go, the water rises.'

At first he thought this was a joke. Windbreaker was making fun of the tour guide, of his dour litany concerning sea levels.

But then Windbreaker hadn't been in the lobby for that, and was raising his voice now and glaring and half-shouting, 'We cannot wait, the water!' and he realized with a start the man was referring to the tide and perfectly serious.

'My wife's in the restroom,' he answered. 'We still have a minute, right?'

'It has to go.' Losing faith in his English or his ability to persuade, Windbreaker turned to the front-desk clerk and laid down a cover fire of Italian and headed for the door. The clerk spoke even as his friend was exiting.

'Sir, the boat has to leave. The water rises too fast. If they wait longer, they are sticking under the bridge. They cannot go.'

He followed his wife's example, talking while moving across the lobby to evade resistance. 'My wife, she's almost done. Just two seconds,' as he strode around the tour group to the corner with the women's restroom.

He knocked plenty of times and called her name plenty more, and silence. This counted in tourist terms as an emergency. He opened the restroom door and poked his head in and called again. She wasn't in there. But she hadn't come back into the lobby, either. Had she gone directly outside, not toward him but toward the door, thinking he was already on the boat, and he'd missed her?

He ran toward the door and crashed into Windbreaker, jogging in yet again to announce their departure, and Windbreaker said, 'Good, we go, it has to go,' and took him by the arm and he asked Windbreaker, 'Is she on there?' and the water was so close to the door, it took only three steps to cross the landing and Windbreaker said unresponsively over the engine noise, 'There are many seats.' The two men hopped on deck and he ducked his head into the main cabin and saw arranged around the mahogany horseshoe bench a woman with museum-benefit hair and two long sons; an Asian male in his twenties with a backpack; and the Englishman from the elevator, showing his nose some mercy. His wife was not on the boat.

They had launched and progressed by the time he could make understood his predicament. It took eight minutes to get him somewhere he could take a water taxi back. The woman and her sons were from North Carolina, the young Asian fellow from just outside Osaka. He must have been in the elevator, too—he and the Englishman were together, and how else would he have pegged the Englishman without hearing him talk to someone—but he did not remember him. The Englishman stayed close to his Japanese friend, and got little in return. His friend threw broken sticks of English at the teenagers and presented them with Japanese coins and postcards he produced endlessly from a fannypack. Each time the Englishman moved closer, and regarded the teenagers as pretext to stay involved and stay close, Osaka ranged farther. Each time the teenagers tried to return a coin or postcard after nominal examination, Osaka pushed it back in the universal language of gifting. These transactions were painful to watch; the Englishman kept a dogged cheer, and the teenagers gave each other more looks than there were zippered pockets in a Japanese fannypack.

Maybe his wife was in one of those pockets.

Back at the hotel there was no sign of the ogling clerk. There was instead a young woman behind the front desk, tending alertly to a computer printer at thigh height. She seemed competent, the kind who would never dream of returning tuxedoes late. He described his wife. She hadn't seen her. He used the desk phone to call up to the room. The woman wore a gold nameplate reading TEODORA, pinned distractingly on her blouse at the very nipple end of her left breast. This suggested to him a cartoonist's depiction of a boob sparkling in the sun. Or a nursing infant somewhere with a rectangular mouth. Or an indifference that was either innocent or disdainful. He let it ring and ring. No answer.

As he listened, lulled by the burbling European tones, he found himself considering Teodora and himself as children growing up together, neighbors but not schoolmates, a small accidental friendship of hiding under hedges and telling each other funny things that friends the other didn't know had said. How there would have been time by now to betray each other more than once and recover, only before losing touch altogether, and not a single third person to prove this part of their lives had ever happened. As he pressed the phone to his head, Teodora neither smiled nor frowned, and when he hung up and asked if he could leave a note for his wife, she barked 'Of course' so sharply that his startled hand made a clattering mess of the phone and its cradle.

He scoured the lobby. A girl of what looked about sixteen sat on a sofa scowling down at a newspaper folded the wrong way, top halves of both pages showing and bottom halves tucked under, so it spread across her lap like a sideboard. He described his wife, but she hadn't seen her.

He went back to the women's restroom, knocked, called out. Nothing. For good measure he checked the men's restroom, washed his hands. He left the restroom and noted this offshoot corridor held only the two restrooms. She would have had to pass out of it back into the lobby.

The hotel restaurant.

He went there and explained his circumstance to a waiter tending tables near the restaurant entrance. This sheepish type was cowed further by the prospect of stepping in for the absent hostess. 'At your service,' the waiter said, motionless. Please do not flay me alive, the waiter's eyes said, blinkless.

He pushed past the waiter and looked around himself."

He hiked up his elbows when typing. He canted his wrists so each hand bladed down from above. It was how a marionette might type. It felt ridiculous. Likely it looked ridiculous, too. But no one else saw. He hadn't had anybody over in months. Years?

Classic discipline. It worked for the same reason Titian painted with the canvas rotated ninety degrees, and Piranesi favored parallel lines over cross-hatches for shading. Making it harder made it better. Now each finger reached out deliberately and with full motion. He was plucking at individual keys, not hammering blindly in their vicinities.

The tempering effect was immediate. His sentences steadied. His scenes shook off their spasm and bloomed.

But his fingers felt insubstantial, inconsequential. Without the meat of his hands to ground them, they didn't move so much as shiver. They came down out of the air like precipitation, and when did eight raindrops change anything?

"Looking for someone in a strange place is like listening at the symphony for breathing. Folly. Too little amid too much. The distractions pour over the face, stream around the head, wash away concentration and even the notion of concentrating. Everything is novel and therefore notable. There is no triage between importance and garbage. Numbness reigns.

All that day he traveled, laying his course by the rounding sun. He had no idea where she could have gone. A piece of the sky threatened, and it began misting once. But honest rain never fell. How many times did he walk down a fantastically narrow street and brace with both hands against the walls and push there with all frustration? Not enough that he left any trace on the skin. Enough that he felt the bruise in his bones, the four above each palm at the base of the fingers. Ellipses with an extra dot to make exceptionally sure he did not miss their meaning. When the streets opened to saner widths, he walked with his hands pressed together in front of him. Each pain merged there with its counterpart pain. He pressed tight as a priority only at the palms so that the fingers wandered and made prayerful hands in a careless way. He walked with these hands along the makeshift trail of wooden platforms snaking across the Piazza San Marco at 100 centimeters in the air, above the standing water, the *passerelle* he'd heard it called, and he was certain others suspected the hands were for balance, and he was certain they should mind their own business.

The streets were strangely empty. Against a vacant storefront stood two men chatting. One held a cigarette. The other gestured with what had to be an empty briefcase.

Later, behind the train station, a boy approached. The boy used small steps, measured steps, self-conscious, as if not wanting to wake anyone. Another boy stood off, leaning against a peeling yellow wall, watching.

'Fammi vedere la tua forza,' said the younger boy. Let me see your force. Let me see your strength.

The boy's look did not hold. He eyed the ground, and kept his hands pressed flat and stiff against the sides of his thighs. The result was a weird mix of hopeful and disheartened.

'Mi forza?' he repeated.

The boy nodded.

He hadn't thought his own appearance very different from that of the Italian men he'd passed in the streets. But American men, with their stature and gym habits, were said to stand out in southern Europe. The boy's curiosity was understandable.

Slowly he unbuttoned one shirt cuff, giving the boy a slow grin. The boy did not react. Before continuing, he raised a finger level with the boy's face and said, 'Cuidado, ahora, tener cuidado!' but there was nothing lighthearted about the boy, and at a loss for what else he could do to build up to the moment, he simply rolled up his sleeve and flexed his bicep.

'Grande, verdad? Muy fuerte. Estoy muy fuerte.'

The boy stood staring. The other boy, the one at a distance, only shifted in place, switching the foot braced against the wall behind him.

'Ahora déjame ver *tu* forza,' he said.

The boy, cautious before, now was nothing tentative. The boy grasped at the sleeve of his short-sleeved shirt and whipped it over his shoulder and flexed his arm until a breakfast sausage stood out quivering.

He broke into raucous applause. 'Primer premio, primer premio! Tú estás muy, muy fuerte, *más* fuerte!' The boy received a clap on the shoulder with aplomb, still flexing, still grave, gritting his teeth in frozen discipline, still staring at his own bicep.

He went into his wallet. He had not yet changed money. Only U.S. twenties. He fished one out and held it toward the boy. The boy started running even before plucking it out of his hand. An instant and he had joined the older boy, and the two of them looked back at him briefly, matter-of-factly, confirming his whereabouts before taking their leave, and scampered out of sight.

Each time he was sure he was lost, he drew comfort from the idea that linear progress was a certainty, that steady increments in a direction ineluctably yield a destination. And then the street he was following would drop into a canal, or end in a blank wall. No recourse but to double back, no one around to appreciate how exasperated the skrutch of his about-face. These broken lines he was treading were just long enough to let him pretend there was progress. A loop, involuted and pointless and endless.

He remembered their first time. One long kiss throughout. She'd laid her hand alongside their mouths. This hand did not caress. It guarded. Part of it touched her cheek, part of it his. It walled off the air where their mouths joined. The palm was irrelevant. The way L. held it made clear the back of this hand was what mattered. The way a starving prisoner shields his plate. This was greed. Love was just a kind of greed. This woman loved him.

The first time with his wife there was a window open. He had not wanted to seem inconsiderate for doing nothing about the chill. He had not wished to seem inattentive for ministering to a window. It stayed open. A bead of sweat purling down the gully of his back. That is what he remembered. And a car horn.

A dog barked somewhere. At the same moment a waft of rot passed through. The heavy afternoon connected them. The dog had found something dead. Or death had jammed like a chicken bone in the dog's throat and dislodged barkward.

He found himself wondering if he'd run into them and, if so, whether the Japanese would lead as they walked the platforms and the Englishman come pining after, or whether the Englishman would go ahead, full of excited talk, his friend lagging behind, looking off at something he was missing, noting to visit it later, alone, with someone else.

He stopped to carve her initials and his into a white wall. The surface had a legume feel—new paint—and shone like a beggar's blind eye. The raw bright of it encouraged the failing sunlight. He scored the letters carefully, ditch after little ditch. The dark gray underneath showed up eagerly. The encircling heart would be the biggest challenge. It would mean some mileage for his thumbnail. If the initials were scored neatly and deeply enough, he could keep them small. He had just finished inscribing both pairs of letters when it occurred to him that this wall was not simply the side of the street, but the side of someone's house, he was defacing someone's home, and at this very moment, his hand leavening the air with palsies of indecision, the dog came ripping around the corner bounding straight at him and he heard it panting and scrabbling but otherwise making no noise and this last was the most terrifying sound of all. He ran and jumped a wall and crossed a bridge and ran.

He lost the dog, and himself for good measure. Asking directions was no help. These confirmed the major sense he'd already had of where he was headed, but without precision enough to override his minor, and poor, instincts about how to get there.

He had in mind that he hadn't carved a plus sign between the pairs of initials because his plan had been to do a heart around them instead. But now he realized there was no either-or: everybody knew you did a plus sign *and* a heart. So now he was left with no good reason for having left an almost certainly inaccurate manifest on the side of a stranger's home.

He made his way through a *campo*. They had thousands of these squares, it seemed. Thousands, and maybe a total of three benches among them. This square was medium-sized. Ten streetlamps, five on either side of a path. Only two working. He smelled cigarette smoke, heard a thin laugh. Shifting figures in the darkness. A woman's voice, calling out to him.

'Fammi vedere la tua forza?'

He tried to make out which body was saying this, then considered that peering could only incite. He kept walking.

The skritch of high heels on worn concrete. Tittering.

'Cara, dove stai andando? *Fammi vedere la tua forza.*'

Let me see your force. Let me see your manhood."

Every day he whittled. For hours. He tired out his fingers before typing a single word. Heavy with the organic weight of their own depletion, he thought, his fingers would hang and move with import: pendula driving a landed family's hoard of clocks; medallions glinting the breasts of two brothers back from war.

He let his palm help with the knife. This felt louche. For penance he never let the knife rest while he held it. Each morning started with a block of wood. By noontime the kitchen table teemed with toothpicks.

He loved the first half of the regimen, when smaller choppings emerged, looking like the same little-titted woman with shoulder-length hair. The latter half, when he was obliged to go smaller and split these intermediate figures, he liked less.

Once done, he did not wait to clear it. He slapped down his computer on top of the skittering mess. It felt like laying out a picnic blanket in a cut hayfield. Except there was nothing good to eat, because he worked through lunchtime.

Things shaped up and things didn't. His fingers indeed dragged. Regrettably the prose dragged, too. It drowsed on the brink of action, luxuriated over settings without ever lighting out. It ambled through interior monologue when it should have raced. It didn't tell a story; it curled up in bed waiting for one.

"By the time he got back, it was dark. He'd had nothing to eat but the spit in his mouth. The moonlight was tentative. The hotel lost its corners in it. Home for now was a furry bulk, a halt and humped-over creature. The kind that's lost too many fights. Its back was the color of loam and whisper.

When he entered, he went straight for the front desk. He'd go up to the room next, in case his wife had returned. But first he'd check for messages.

There was no one behind the front desk. He looked around. The lobby was empty. The button bell produced nothing except an especially breathy ting. He thought about writing a note, but a message about messages hurt his head. He'd give it a couple of minutes.

What time was it? He had left his watch in the room that morning. There was a clock in the lobby near the seating area. He guessed it was seven or eight o'clock. But here, the clock—it couldn't be right. It read three o'clock. But it was dark outside.

Three A.M.? That didn't make sense. He had not been wandering for fifteen hours. He did not feel at all tired. Well, his limbs were sore. But his head was calm. Gauzy, but relaxed.

He directed himself to the corner with the restrooms. Diagonally, and through the carpeted seating area, so that his footsteps went silent before calling out again. He turned the corner. Walked past one restroom. Walked past the other. Was about to turn back when he remembered he was now in the business of giving it time, and so walked the remaining length of the corridor, slowly, one foot in front of the other as if still on the yawning plaza's passerelle, one hand on each wall as if still in the choking streets. Ten mongrel meters of dry and fragrant and perfectly lonely impossibility.

He turned back to where the corridor began at the lobby—still no clerk—and like a child starting a game right, he began again, a hand against each wall. His left ran over the ribbed door frame preceding the women's restroom, an increasingly protruding series, the lateral equivalent of steps up to a great hall. Fingers climbed while thumb presided. At the far side of the door frame, there was no gradual passage down, just a leap from the top step. His fingers did the same against the door frame on either side of the men's restroom: an awed ascent, a careless launch.

What's this? His stomach shifted. It would have been something had he felt with his innocent right hand the break in the corridor wall. It would have been something if rather than seeing it, he had instead read with his eyes closed, with his palm, the corridor giving way to a narrower passageway that turned sharply to the right. But this was not a story. This was not a dream. He had made a mistake. The corridor was not a dead end at all. When he'd looked this morning, he hadn't seen the passageway. The light from the lobby had been too weak to relief against the back wall the edge of the side wall where it stopped. He hopped off his imposserelle. He turned the corner.

At the other end of this narrower corridor he saw a door. Above it was a green-and-white sign reading USCITA with a stick figure running after an arrow into a dark rectangle. A hidden exit. He had stood in the lobby for how long on the assumption his wife would have had to exit his way. And he'd been wrong. But here, suddenly, at his right elbow: a second door off this new hidden hallway. It was already open a few inches. Wedged open by a white painted brick resting on its side. He nudged the door an inch wider and peered inside.

The first thing he saw was the ogling clerk. The clerk stood a few feet away, in the center of the room, his back toward the door, his pants at his calves. That muss of hair was unmistakable. The clerk's ass was bare. No shirttail to cover it. He was wearing a kind of half-shirt. No, the clerk had gathered his shirt and tucked it under itself at the navel, to get it out of the way.

The clerk was in mid-fuck. His efforts were directed at a table, or someone on a table, at thigh height."

He bent a toothpick until it split open and showed its bones. He wrapped it around his index finger, keeping the jagged break on the side so that it pricked the meat of the next digit too, and with a tab of duct tape connected the tips. He did this seven more times.

Pain, small and specific. Like laggard horses to the crop, the fingers responded. Words ripped from one thought to the next. Paragraphs touched ground long enough to orient the reader and no longer, galloping to the next thing. The verbs soared. The nouns stayed out of the goddamn way.

What happened next shouldn't have been a surprise. The other cures had spoiled, too, after working awhile. Now, this one lost none of its advantage. His writing still moved strong and liquid. But the words carried with them a dark silt of provocation and meanness and cruelty. More and more they sounded like someone else's, someone whom after the briefest conversation he decidedly would not like.

He was not by nature a cynical man. It was the fingers. They were to blame. Miring each other in small agonies—partly inured by them, partly desperate to distract from them—his fingers were authoring larger ones.

He hated what was happening.

But people loved it.

So much so that he risked disrespect by referring to them in public as "people" rather than "my readers." So many that he increasingly had occasion to refer to them in public.

He stuck to his regimen, notwithstanding the time and contrivance required. Arts-and-crafts for artist's craft. After donning his spurs, he always turned off the phone. He didn't want to talk to people the same way he was writing for them.

One afternoon he forgot. He ignored the rings. When the second call came, he pinkied the speaker button.

Yes? The spurs made him gruff.

The gruffness made her still more curt, businesslike.

It had been a long time. Yes, yes, it had. How was he? Good, he was good. How was she? Good, good.

Then she said: *There is something I need to talk to you about.*

On his way to the coffee shop he reviewed. She had not said *I have something*, but *There is something*. What she wished to discuss was not some trifling fancy, but something substantial, something mutually meaningful. Something affecting the both of them. Also she had not said *I want to talk to you about*, or even *we should talk about*. She needed to talk about this. She had private feelings, urgent feelings. It was an entreaty after all. She needed. A heartfelt plea really.

On entering the coffee shop, he spotted her immediately. At a table, looking down, considering the backs of her hands.

She got up when she saw him. On its way his ass disturbed the backs of chairs. She looked down at her own chair as she extended a hand. Plainly she worried either that the chair would float away or that he would try a hug. Neither developed.

Hi, there.

Hi.

They sat. He looked affably at the next table, then back at her with his Robert Wagnerest smile.

Having anything? he ventured.

No one's having anything, she said. *Except a talk. Once we're done, and I'm gone, you can order five whipped creams with whipped cream. Right now we're going to talk.*

He had the look of a man freshly slapped with a wrench.

What—

She didn't let him finish.

How long has it been since the last time we saw each other? she asked.

I don't know.

She simply stared. As if she'd stopped considering the backs of her hands only to consider using them.

He shifted in his seat. *Four years? Five years?*

Five years. That's funny. Because I've seen you a lot since then. Shop-and-Save, two weeks ago. A month ago, the salad place across from my office. Nothing?

He cocked his head. Absent another strategy, moving his ear away from the words was worth a try.

Let's put it this way, she said. *When I got pneumonia in February and went in the hospital, what was the first thing I told the nurse? Not my medications. Not that my sister was on her way. I gave her your description. I told her not to let you in if you showed up. I took my oxygen off to tell her that.*

Okay, he said.

Not okay. Her lips moved around the words like punches. *You cannot lurk around, follow me everywhere. I see you again, I call the police. Period. Don't care if we're at the same funeral. You see me coming, go the other way. Run. Because I'm calling the police. Do you understand?*

His head was down. She felt sorry but she willed herself to ignore that.

She stood up.

I have to let you go first, she said.

He knew she meant, *I have to watch you go before I can go.*

He knew she really meant, *I have to let go of you before I can go on.*

Forty minutes later, hunched against a garbage can that

smelled of poo and factories, he heard her overhead, the desultory skretch of tired heels on concrete, climbing the stairs outside her brownstone.

He was done sitting there. He would come out and present himself. He would just tell her finally how she was his.

Anyone sitting here? A young woman stood over the table, indicating the other chair, which was empty. She held a cup of coffee in one hand, a backpack in the other. Her eyebrows showed she'd asked more than once. Her backpack drooped long like a line of caught fish.

No, of course, he said. *Please.*

She set the coffee down hard. She didn't see the pile of stirrers, which skittered everywhere.

As the young woman sat down and arranged herself, and put on a cycling cap, he settled in for more daydreams. Never in his life had he stalked anyone. Never in his life had he dared. He pretended not to notice her turn the cap backward. He wondered what luck in life, what boldness, a Euro-gangstress hat might confer on its wearer. He considered which required the less character: failing to muster the courage, or failing to disgust oneself entirely for wanting to.

"The room was dim. The only light was from a single bulb hanging in an open closet. If he was at the southeast corner of the room, the bulb hung in the southwest corner. He and the bulb formed a triangle with the clerk's laboring ass, northward. The bulb, confident and specially in his sightline, seemed to be saying to him, Are you seeing this? Are you getting this?

The clerk used a strange motion, standing straight and bending forward at the hips, so that his body was a line and then a curve and then a line again. There was no crouch to his hips, no brace to his legs. His face and chest were upright, uninvested in his progress. It was the aimless what-do-you-know motion of someone waiting for a bus and growing restless. It was a loping in place.

Then he saw them. Two legs, one dangling on each side of the clerk. Stunted brackets around a pulsing parenthesis. A woman lying face-up on the table, but all he could see were legs, not gathered up on the table but rather left loose like that.

Two things blew into his head at once and merged there and seared.

It was careless and self-abandoning and profoundly shameful the way these legs dangled.

And these legs ended in a pair of slate-gray Mary Janes.

Not a sound. There wasn't a sound in here. His wife wasn't making a sound.

He picked up the brick at his feet and lifted it and it was heavier than he thought it would be. Awkward with the knowledge that there was no good side to this brick or to what he was about to do, bold with the merely observed, unapologetic certainty that the violence he felt would swell much, much bigger once it got outside of him, martially indignant that the slightest surprise to this man without making it fatal might startle him into ejaculating into his new wife and that was unacceptable, he lifted the brick

and less of it slammed into the side of the clerk's head than he'd intended, in fact only an edge of the brick made contact, but it turned out even better because it made a kind of stonecutting contact with the hollow at the temple and sent the clerk crumpling down where he stood as if he'd meant to pour himself like a warm batter atop the bunched circle of his pants.

He stepped around to his wife.

This was not his wife.

This was the other clerk. This was Teodora.

Her shirt was rolled tightly across her upper chest at the armpits. Awning and loiterers underneath and neither ending in a brilliant rectangle. She brought up her bare legs, horrified. She was scrabbling backward on the table but, whether because of her panic or her shoes getting little purchase, made little progress and only shished against the surface of the table, this sound the first he'd heard since he'd looked into this hellroom, her eyes wide but her mouth tight as if the rest of her were wondering what to do or judging something or judging that wondering what to do would get her nowhere.

The second sound was a sharp yelp she made, a trial scream, stifled by terror. She would shake off that paralysis soon, he knew, and when he put his hand out to quiet her, this happened: she bit him with impossible quickness and a snap of her neck, and as quickly released, because then with her right foot she gave a jagged lucky kick that crashed against his chin like a brickbat. His knees nearly buckled at the same moment as he saw her teeth clench her bottom lip and he put out his left arm and blocked her leg when it tried again.

His right was also in motion. The brick made such complete contact, it was as if the brick and her forehead had once been two halves of the same block and the moment of their original fission was rewound. Twice wrong, because when he thought the man would resist that first glancing blow, the man toppled instead, and when he thought with alarm the woman was finished, she persevered. For such a large and perfect impact, the result was minuscule. She still grasped both sides of the table, but now sat frozen, her head off by itself, cocked away from him, eyes closed, bracing for the next blow, also hiding in plain sight, it seemed, and hoping to escape notice.

The next blow was awkward, extended out from his body, a swatting. This time he heard a splintering from under the brick when it came down—no series of sounds, just a single funch. She curled off the table onto the floor in segments. It was the side of the table away from him, so he went around.

Black Mary Janes. Worn, though. Scuffed.

He vomited twice. A flitting through his head said he was not responsible for this because he hadn't eaten anything that day, and the mud that filled behind it confused which barbarity he was not responsible for.

Without wiping his mouth he went to the door and crouched there, listening. He didn't hear anything. These practical movements cleared some of the mud. The possibility of a security camera occurred to him. Even before he glanced around and saw none, he understood he didn't need to rise out of his crouch to look more thoroughly. The clerks would not have come here if there were a camera.

He put a hand as gently as he could on the door handle. Not a knob, but a lever, a stainless steel chiding: this was not a room for frolic. The lever did not give. He tried pulling up instead of pushing down. Nothing. He stood up finally and yanked both ways like a boy, fast, but the handle was fixed in place. He was locked in. He realized that's what the brick had been for–to keep from getting locked in. What kind of hotel had utility rooms that locked on both sides? There was no visible space between door and door frame, but it felt like a deadbolt. He was trapped.

He moved sideways toward the corner closet with his back to the wall, intent on not looking down–with small steps, measured steps, because all he could think of was bodies. In the closet were shelves with folded clean pillowcases, and a wheeled canvas cart holding unfolded bedsheets. He picked up a sheet. It was not visibly soiled. But from its neutral smell he deduced it had not been laundered.

Bodies, tender and splayed. Every sprawl and convexity in them was a bluff. They wanted to show how strong they were just when they were feeblest.

He picked up more sheets and covered them. With the man he teamed with nose and toes and forced the sheet into tautness. The woman lay on her side, and it was one thing to cover a body when supine, entirely another when it could be curled up on a couch in wintertime, sky outside giving in, the serene smell of furnace heat, voices from the kitchen.

Back in the closet, what occurred to him was the nesting pieceness of things. Venice, a reek-filled piece of the world, and a faithful one for both the two-thirds water and the stench; the hotel, an improbably scented piece of Venice; this room, inert and obscure, inside the hotel; the closet inside the room; his body inside the closet. Inside his body, furnace heat and voices.

This thought should have been satisfying. It had seriality, congruence. But it was not satisfying at all. It occurred to him there must be something more. A linear progression starting with the world and stopping with him. It seemed specious and inelegant. Out of ouder. There must be something more, something inside him, something that would preserve the endless loop of things.

He was still holding a bedsheet. An impulse to tear it lengthwise, and he did. It tore easily."

His last undertaking was the simplest: a stick. It was a lozenge of gray-brown, squat and pale and porous. He let it rest like a troll's bridge across the tops of his hands while he typed. It looked a little like jerky, nibbled; a little like coin wrappers, wadded.

The writing: daring but not frivolous, vigorous yet equable, profound but not ponderous. Each page read as if were inexorable. There are more prudent descriptions, ones that do not clamor for doubt. Only one is true. The writing was perfect.

His accomplishments mounted, and his fame grew. He did not draw attention to the stick. Certainly he did not announce his use of it. But a man with pupils and admirers and, increasingly, romantic involvements is soon pried from his privacies. The object was so simple and strange, and the way it rode his hands so singular, that it fueled a cultural obsession. It was a balance beam, some said, letting his hands work freely but always smoothly. Others insisted the stick's power was symbolic, representing a merger of two incommensurates: the solid, the precarious. Then there were those who maintained it wasn't a stick at all: it was Hemingway's partly smoked cigar, discovered posthumously alongside a buffalo-horn knuckleduster; a meteorite, made of metals not found on this earth and punished into length by a jealous atmosphere; the dowel on a hotel key, set down by one of his characters on the floor of a linen closet after emptying his pockets.

At interviews they always asked. He answered with a poise that cowed them from noting he'd answered a different question.

At readings they never asked. The questioners were two kinds: striving and merely wanting to air their cleverness, or earnest and merely wanting from him more than he'd written.

One afternoon the phone rang. It was not, as expected, his agent confirming a reading.

It was her.

On his way to the coffee shop he reviewed. She had not said *I have something*, but *There is* something. Clearly she wished to talk about something substantial, something affecting the both of them. She *needed* to talk about this, is what she said. This was urgency. This was a plea.

On entering the coffee shop, he spotted her immediately. At a table, concerned with a book. Her shoulders perched small and round: handfuls.

She got up when she saw him. On its way his ass disturbed the backs of chairs. The hug was polite but long enough for him to smell soap. Vetiver. He sat down and folded his arms so his hands wouldn't show.

They appraised each other during small talk, playing the middle-aged trick of casting glances elsewhere to deflect suspicions of gawking but, when the eye contact finally came, taking full advantage. Her gray eyes, her lovely ears. That hair could not hide her ears from him. He remembered how it felt to send whispers down those velvet circling culverts. He remembered how these liplike riblets of skin kissed back.

Don't be weird, she said.

What? he said. I was being weird, his eyebrows said.

Standing in line for coffee, they didn't speak. She looked nothing as nervous as he felt. Sitting down again, they talked about how she was considering going back to school; how things with him were pretty great; how renting a floor of a brownstone made so much more sense than her previous apartment; how his writing was going well, imagine that; how she hurt her ankle during a drive to Boston just from hovering it over the accelerator for so long; how brownstone owners with kids always set furnaces for plenty of heat in winter; how she realized a few weeks ago while talking to a girlfriend that she'd never gotten back those two semesters of his tuition she'd paid for before they got married, and not a big deal but that would be nice to have, which he said would be no problem of course; how for exercise she swam every day; how, was this right, she now lived only about an hour from him; how the steroids for her ankle made her feel invincible, made swimming feel like she was eating the world with her arms; how, no, closer to two.

"Action. Zeal. Always do. He dropped the torn pieces of bedsheet where he stood. He walked to the door. It looked blankly back. A hard kick would accomplish little, because the door opened into the room, and so kicking out would only wedge it against the door frame. Plus someone might hear and discover him.

Always do. He would be discovered one way or the other.

He gave the door a severe kick. Nothing. He was right. He was kicking the wrong way. The door opened into the room, not the corridor outside.

Another kick, this one devastating. The door bounced off the wood against which it nested and came back and idled loose in the door frame. Now there was a full inch of give between the door fully pulled toward him and the door pushed back in its frame. He grabbed the door handle and wrenched toward him, yanked back and forth. Almost.

A third kick and again the door turned henchman and on his behalf did all sorts of damage to the frame. The cracking sounds were huffy, asthmatic. Old wood. He tugged back and forth and, still holding the door, he fell into the wall alongside, opening the door suddenly and wide with the weight of his stumbling body.

He peered into the corridor. To his right was the exit. To the left was the lobby. He heard nothing from either direction. His throat tightened. He pulled the door behind him; it met the frame and floated away again. He made his way to the lobby, rapidly, and could not help thinking that his feet were making a mess of things. He tried not to think about his invisible passerelle, but it was hard. He tried thinking instead how it'd be no big deal if he were shin-deep in fetid standing water because he was headed directly to sanctuary and fresh socks, to where he could laugh with her.

'Cold feet are before the wedding.'

'They're wet, not cold.'

'Wedding's come and gone,' she'd reply, ignoring him. 'Too late now, bitch.'

The lobby was empty still. He walked quickly but without outward sign of anxiety. He pretended he was five minutes late for coffee with a friend. The result, should someone observe him, would project a sweet spot—neither pleasantly approachable nor suspiciously nervous. One elevator waited with its doors open, the same one out of service that morning. He got in and pressed a button and the doors closed.

It was the carpet's pile underfoot, or the gasp from the closing doors. Something made him think of it. The special anguish when something gentle gets broken. He came home that day. L. had found out. She looked at him as if there was no air where she was. In the realm of anecdote, of banter, cheating on someone with a future spouse is absolved. Indeed it earns a kind of bonhomie credit. The offense in hindsight is a footfault, a tax dutifully—charmingly—paid for the privilege of living life fully. No credit here. First, he would never tell the anecdote. It didn't tell like an anecdote. It told like a pair of knives: She was everything. He lost everything. Second, he could never tell it anyway. You don't chuckle about devastation. Years ago it occurred to him about that hand. It wasn't for greed. It was for whispering. It was the exact hand you put at someone's ear to tell a secret. That kiss told a secret, and no less a secret for knowing it already: He'd never love anyone like that again.

At the hotel room he knocked. He listened. He heard nothing. He went into his pocket for the room key. Empty. The other pocket was empty, too. Alarmed, he felt for his wallet in his back pocket. It was there all right, but no key anywhere.

He tried the door. The knob turned easily. The door swung softly in.

His wife, in bed, shifted to look at him. The lights were on. But she'd been asleep. His noise had woken her. Though her head was turned, her body remained elegantly flat under the bedsheet, enjoying its rest.

'Honey, you're home,' she sang softly.

'Are you okay?'

'Little better.' She yawned. 'Sorry about leaving you in the lobby. I felt horrible. I couldn't find you and went back up to the room. What time is it?'

Two windows hung over the other side of the bed. The blind on one was shut tight. The window at the foot of the bed had its blind open. The moon shone there. It watched him as he watched it, both of them knowing she couldn't see it. It was saying, Do you see her there? Will you go to her there?

'I looked everywhere for you.' He closed the door behind him. 'How'd you get in?'

'God,' she said, stirring, 'is it dark outside?'

'How'd you get in the room?'

'They use things in this country called keys.' She let her hand fall lightly onto the night table and the sumptuous room key lying there.

He went to her and put his fists into the mattress alongside her shoulders and smiled down into her gray eyes.

'So the Italian word for key is "key"?' he said, low and soft. 'What are the chances?'

'The chances are exactly zero of you getting in this bed,' she chirped, which meant she wanted to giggle but wasn't letting herself. 'That kind of attitude.'

He took off nothing and got under the bedsheet and into her arms."

The coffee was gone. The tables nearby were empty. Her eyes, mostly down, were up again, and some of their smile had spilled.

The young writers were copying him. On their hands teetered all manner of miscellanea longer than wide: relay batons, cockpit levers, headless gavels, door hangers barking (NON DISTURBARE), dagger blades, rifle scopes, bloodless thermometers, door hangers begging (RIFARE LA CAMERA), fish spines, lion quills, doorless knockers, vetiver stalks.

Was there something, he asked, *you needed to talk to me about?*

The old writers, against the caution of a lifetime of things not mattering much after all, talked of him.

We just did, she said. *About the tuition?*

"They took him down carefully. There was little space in the closet to maneuver. They did not notice the mark. It was halfway down the length of sheet, a faded line—a scratch, from a thumbnail.

One of them, on a chair, worked a bad knife against the cotton, slowly, because the weight would fall dumb and sudden. Even this one did not notice. They braced, and caught, and spat a few words. They laid down as gently as brute weight allowed.

No one saw how despair had yielded, too late, to love and thoughts of love."

***

None of them—not the pupils nor the admirers, the imitators, the lovers—noticed the curious seam that ran across the middle of the stick. Nor did they make out the glassy patches at both ends, or the half-moons nestled there.

He did not ask what was in Boston because he had a feeling.

None of them would have believed what the stick was had he told them.

This hug was even shorter. This time he smelled nothing. Not breathing in was the most important part of not letting anything out.

They did not know these thumbs moved their once and current bearer, each time he sat down to create whole worlds, by sheer reminder of how much he'd lost, to prove their little moons were on the rise, giving light to prevail by.

OF SATISFACTION AND
THE LYING SUN

THE NIGHT HE LOST HIS WIFE, BEFORE THE DIVORCE WAS FINAL, or filed, or a word uttered with intent in their kitchen–that is, the night his wife decided that she could not go on like this and that a divorce was in order–he had been researching the doctrine of satisfaction of antecedent debt. The case law was solid. So were his doubts. Even as he drafted the brief, he had wondered, perhaps virile with the protein of delivery sushi, perhaps ornery from the nighttime chill pouring off his office window, why the argument made sense. He wondered why the mere existence of a contract would entitle his creditor-client to retain payments from a bankrupt, when simple payments for goods delivered or services rendered would not. He liked the argument. Indeed, he needed it. It felt, however, slippery.

The day his ex-wife and son were in a car accident, he was traveling for a deposition. American Airlines Flight 10 from JFK to LAX. Whereon the Chinese gentleman across the aisle, hearing the flight attendant recite the beer options in the style of one addressing a deaf person, blinked, and examined the back of the seat in front of him, and hearing them a second time interrupted after Budweiser to wince like a man with a nail in his kneecap and to growl "Weiser, no weiser" and to point with a fresh definitiveness at the carafe of water atop her cart. He wasn't even taking the deposition that day. He was arriving a day early so he could go over his deposition outline, order room service on the client, eat room service on the client, review the x most important documents yet again with his deposition-exhibit-notating green pen in hand, and surf premium channels so he could plunge himself into the yth episode of a television series he'd not seen before because the vacuum of feeling about the characters and exactly no comprehension of the plot would give him room to enjoy pretending this was among the functionally infinite things he might do all the time if he had the time, if he had a normal life where work did not sit on his head like z, a glum fat person, who though fat was exceedingly fidgety, and who though fidgety, which might suggest a kind of nervous readiness to engage, was nevertheless glumly uncommunicative.

The night his son died, he was at the side of his bed. He had stayed there without a shower or a proper night's sleep since arriving. Initially the humid discomfort was a comfort, or at least a soothing penance, as when one bites down hard on a gratifyingly unyielding pencil with the tooth that aches. After two days he had begun to smell like clay and shallots. While the suffering part of him did not care, the hoping part reveled a bit because something so solemn as death seemed impossible in a place lousy with ordinariness. So the odor was helping, as was the bedside table with the paper cup crumpled on one side and pouty on the other. Also the news on the overhead television kept at a sidebar volume so that every singsong sentence from the anchors seemed as if it should start, "By the way," "By the way." That was helping, and the daylight on the fourth morning streaming in and turning everything into a pastry version of itself. He was not aware of the pain in his left arm. He was praying, but— it turned out—praying in the strictly shallow way that self-consciousness allows, and with all the thin and sagging vigor that comes of hedging one's bets with the likes of newscasters and a tired cup, and fitfully, between intrusions of cynicism that pulsed like a kick drum, a cadence that said that getting a thing because you'd prayed for it seemed implausible, like insulating payments from bankruptcy recovery only because you'd happened to have a contract in place before receiving them. Also like a contract, it had a limited term, the praying. It worked for four nights, during which his boy did not wake up. But not through the fifth, when they said he never would. The next morning he walked out of the hospital lobby and saw that lying sun and hated it like nothing in his life.

The day his ex-wife died was the day of the accident. Her death was immediate. He learned this at the third-floor nurses' station, from an aide named Bennie, who after realizing with whom she was speaking stood up at the same ponderous rate as she set down her clipboard, so that it seemed as if it were the levering action of the two movements that squeezed the horror out of her mouth. His ex-wife had been wearing a seat belt, but the deluxe wide-cab pickup truck traveling under the conduct of a man who wore a tattoo reading AL-WAYF DRIK IN MODERATIOZZZZ did not so much collide with her vehicle as simply ride rampant over the hood and crush her where she sat. In fact, blood alcohol showed the driver had been sober as a ruled notebook. The theory was he had fallen asleep at the wheel after a double shift at the midtown office building where he worked security, though this theory could not be fully verified for the fact the navy polyesters and thinning hair were now a corpse's. Whether the choking sensation was from having lost her, or from trying not to think he'd lost her, or from reminding himself that the papers were proof he should not suppose that he'd lost her, could not be fully verified for the fact that no prescriptive emotional parameters would even account for how the hollow between her jaw and ear had fit his thumb perfectly.

The night he again felt the pain in his arm, he did not simply become aware of it. He also sensed a familiarity that in turn cued a wan memory of having experienced the same pain the night his son had passed, and of having ignored it, or at least not having been in a position to regard it. And because the pain went away, and because it mortified him that after a stranger killing his son, he could feel something so bullshit as fleeting arm pain, he turned punitively in his bed onto the arm in question and went back to sleep.

The day he went to the hospital was the next morning, when he woke up to a pain in his chest so intense and fulminating he could not move. If a bomb took seven hundred twenty milliseconds to explode completely, from detonation to the point at which the force of the bomb no longer impelled any volume of air, then it felt as if someone had secreted inside his thorax a bomb stuck at millisecond eighty-eight. There had been an initial violence, but the device threatened more, much more, and it was this unfinished incendiary business, this prospect of further rough and sudden expansion, that had made him scream loud enough that his housekeeper heard and came up to the bedroom and with preternatural calm directed herself to the landline and called 911 and then put another pillow under his head and opened his shirt and left and came back and put something wet and cold to his lips. Later he would think back and conclude these were not significant undertakings but, given the very few minutes that it took paramedics to arrive, and given the presence of mind needed for such precise and fluid movements, rather impressive nonetheless.

The night he lost hope, he pushed off his comforter and looked at the clock and touched his feet to the floor and put his mind to what there was to do, and realized that he could not remember, and after a moment realized further that this was not entirely true and that in fact he could remember, and that there was plenty to do, but also understood there was no reason to do it, and realized still further that not remembering and not having a reason to remember were effectively, for purposes of impelling his body, his life, the same thing, and noted this was so purely true that his brain had let that fact govern its wet architecture even if only for the last few moments, and he looked again at the clock and realized that forty minutes had elapsed in the time it had taken him to think these things and determine that there was nothing to have done in that time, which seemed like a double waste, like losing a woman you'd already lost, and not being there for a boy for whom you'd not been there, and as he curled slowly back into bed, and settled, he considered his two legs as he laid them together warm with life and what right they had.

The day he saw his housekeeper there at the sink, he was not thinking. It was an illusion. It was late in the day, evening, and in fact it was the illusion of an illusion, because his ex-wife had never been at that sink. He'd moved there after the divorce. Seven times his ex-wife had waited in the car when she'd come to pick up their son, and only twice had she stepped inside, and he never let himself say to her, "Come inside, come inside," because oh how he wanted her to and so that was the weakness, his prudent adult mind knew, against which he had to steel himself especially. And yet something brutal in his head made him want to see his wife there, at the sink. He moved up behind her and put both his hands on the rim of the sink and the water kept running. He put his chest against her back, her head still down, and she kept washing. He put his lips in her hair and then on her neck, and even as his housekeeper kissed him back she turned her head but not her shoulders. He kissed her all over and unbuttoned her pants and took in her smell and put something wet and warm to his lips and later, in the bed, where during his heart attack he had spit up on his own chin and made with the back of his throat a soft questioning noise over and over, and she had closed her eyes without any squint of concentration and just lightly nodded her head down and very straightforwardly prayed, as if speaking to someone she had just spoken to an hour ago, in the way of an update, like talking to a love she had not lost, part of him realized what she had that he had never had, then, or at his son's side. Part of him realized how

this was done, it was done quietly, no drumbeat, no entitlement, this is how it was done.

The night he woke up was that same night, when he
stood and observed a strange woman's sleeping form. Her
mouth hung half open, past benign absorption, but short of
elation, to a medium point of ardent interest, or of mild surprise, with a slight pursing that spoke an eagerness to believe.
The side of her left breast sloped like the persevering roof on
a shed. His legs, for their part, stood hollow, not simply empty but abloat with smaller empty leg-shaped cavities within,
good places for doubts that might ring like change as he
walked. Which he did, to the corner of the room, where the
two walls met for him, plain and stalwart as day and night.
He fit his back there, pushing harder against the discomfort,
and drew up his legs. He took those two empty spaces in his
arms, and wondered with nothing like definitiveness whether
existing once was cause enough to exist again, and pressed
his knees against his face, which felt, however, slippery.

KENNEDY TRAVEL

ONCE HE SEES HER HE CANNOT STOP LOOKING. UPON AN EXQUISITE left shoulder hangs a purse, and this purse barely moves. A time—early morning—for introspection, for making plans, and here he is, marveling at the speed of a strange woman's walk, and at a purse so calm on her rocketing shoulder it mocks him.

He's hurrying. But she's on the other side of the street already, the same side as the stop. In a few moments she could be boarding the bus. He'd still be teetering on the curb, waiting to cross.

She does not look at him, at anything other than the ground ahead. This makes him feel intrusive and obsessive for looking. He gives up steady observation and tries stealing glances instead. This makes him feel less intrusive and more obsessive.

After a half block it is awkward. Walking in parallel like this. Walking down a very large aisle together.

He does not need women thinking that he choreographs these situations, that he is some stalker who spins grand schemes in a basement lair to the thrum of his mother's washer-dryer. Between glances, rallying against the morning torpor that hangs from the backs of his eyes, he makes an effort to look smartly at the sidewalk, at his own sleeve. Stalkers seem the type to stare dazedly, he thinks, and so a brisk manner will vindicate him. Then he stops thinking this, because he discovers he tends to stare dazedly when thinking.

He slows, leaving longitude between them. Her hair is neither straight nor curly. It is a rich confusion that pours into the hollow between her shoulder blades. Her ass switches crisply back and forth.

The bus arrives. She boards and takes a seat in back. It seems coarse to pursue her a second time. He chooses a seat at a decent remove, near the front. When his stop comes, he permits himself a look. Gone. She must have gotten off earlier, using the rear door.

The next morning, there she is. He walks faster.

As they approach the bus stop, he has time to cross the street and arrive just ahead of her. He does not look at her as he crosses, even though she is within the natural sweep of his vision. He does not turn as he takes those last few steps on the same sidewalk, directly in front of her, to the line of people watching for a bus.

As they wait, he does not give the woman behind him the slightest notice.

Finally, the bus arrives. He shuffles forward with everyone else. When his turn comes to board, he does not proceed. He gets out of the way. He steps to the far side of the door, pivots, faces her, and, silently, gestures with a soft-bladed hand, inclined modestly—not flat, like a serving platter, which might evoke the showy chivalry of the aging bachelor who clowns to make up for balding. He averts his eyes as if to signal he intends only kindness. She boards with a gentle nod but not a word.

Again they sit separately. Again she absconds without him seeing. But he knows the delicious clickitry of her footsteps—so easy to commit to memory that which must be matched and exceeded—and he closes his eyes when he hears it later, seated, too cowardly to turn around, not so cowardly as to permit himself to turn around without engaging.

Day after day this repeats. Against the warm flank of the bus, amid the roar and the reek, he faces her, he indicates with a gentle hand, and she says nothing, moves past, up, wears a little smile. She averts her eyes as if to signal she is accustomed to kindness.

A few mornings he wakes up late. By the time he reaches the sidewalk, she and her jaunty behind are a full block ahead, sometimes two. On these mornings he runs until nearly caught up, then slows on his side of the street to a dignified amble.

One day, when he extends his hand in the usual gesture, she takes it. She leans on it as she takes the first step, lets go as she takes the second.

This is the day he sits next to her.

He does not wish to appear anxious the first time he speaks with her, nor to come off as bothersome during what is likely the quietest part of her day. He does not ask too many questions.

But he learns a lot: that she works at a travel agency, that she came to the United States seven years ago. Her name.

He asks why he never sees her on the bus home. The question is mostly an excuse to speak this new name. *Maybe because we don't ride the same bus home*, she says, smiling at her mischief, and stands, because the bus has reached her stop.

The next morning, he trots out of his apartment building, feeling fresh, and reaches the sidewalk, and does not see her. For the first time in a week he does not see her. He looks at his watch. On time. She must be early. He breaks into a jog, scans for that hair.

With the bus stop in sight, he sees she's not there. He decides she must be lagging this morning. He also decides he'd rather miss the bus than take it without her. But she does not appear. Not for this bus, nor the next. Not the following day, nor the day after. Each bus he boards, he boards reluctantly.

Several days later, he takes the first bus. Too many disappointments have leached him of hope. He takes a window seat, the one she occupied, as he has done the previous days. He does not want to choose between sleeping and looking out the window. He slouches into the sour-smelling nook formed by his seat and the metal of the bus, and halfway through the commute falls into an easy drowse. This is when he sees her.

She is on the sidewalk, on the same side of the street as the bus, but walking in the opposite direction. He looks harder, because he has been half-asleep, and so may be seeing things. She looms, then wisps fast away.

He scrambles to his feet and lurches into the aisle. *Stop!* he shouts and, as if this were meant for himself, halts (mostly) in mid-aisle. He turns back and does something sloppy to the yellow buzz strip. He rolls up the aisle, toward the driver. He hunches down and around; maybe he can glimpse her. He glimpses nothing–a few trees–through the squat and restless skyline of commuters stirring unhelpfully. Finally when the driver brakes, it is with such a pronounced rocking motion that it seems sarcastic: the forward heave a *Happy*, the rearward settling a *Now?* The driver does not look up. A hiss and a serial thud like books dropped onto a shelf as the door opens.

He sees her off in the distance. Rather than call out to her, he runs. He is glad. He is glorious in his gladness. He puts a hand on her shoulder, and speaks her name.

She startles. He apologizes.

She stares. He realizes.

It is not the same woman.

He is silent for too long. She regards him strangely. He will remember this look for decades. For decades he will re-member also the gauze of bewilderment through which he apprehends it. He is silent for too long because realizations are like antique pistols. Reloading requires time. Particularly when one is shaking.

It is not the woman from the bus. It is the woman with whom, years ago, he allowed himself to fall a little in love, before she moved away. It is the woman whose memory he told his head not to excise or jettison or bury, because such measures might themselves embed in his skull's wet filling the dearest bits: how when she held his hand, she held it against her side, and said simply, "Yes," when he joked this was avarice; how she paused on the first words of sentences when hoping to persuade, so that when pleading she called to mind a ringmaster and, when arguing, a slingshot; how she swallowed with her mouth open, like the thirsty and the desperate do, when he was inside her. It is the woman whose memory he instead let surface when it liked, but then passed over benignly, on a high-rustling cumulus of insensibility—in exactly the way the noise of a clerk making change is at once heard and not.

It is the woman.

Twenty-five years later—more than twenty-five years—she remembers. They stumbled into each other on a sidewalk. After so long, she simply turned and, wonderfully, implausibly, there he was. He called her by the wrong name.

Not an altogether unusual name. Pronounced by an American it was unremarkable, three syllables, a suggestion in the last of clinical diagnosis. Perhaps something for a prescription cream. Pronounced in Spanish it was exquisite. Long enough, four syllables, that if heard at all it was hard to mistake. Distinctive enough—first and last syllables the same like ropes on a swing, middle syllables rhyming like a pair of legs working the air—that if heard at all it was hard to forget.

She knows he remembers. She knows how careful the subject of that sidewalk makes him. For a lifetime she has watched his caution. In certain moods it strikes her as gallant and kind; in others she sees the schoolyard runt nursing a scrape no one else can make out.

How they met the first time: dinner out with matchmaking friends, surly waiter, elderly drunk stopping on the way to the restroom to compliment her blouse, gigglish whispers from her tablemates to the left carrying the word "competition" as she thanked the gentleman. No one wants to talk about how they met. It is a story that elicits from listeners a searching, distended look that says, *But get to the part about fate, surely there is a part about fate.*

What they want to talk about, all of them, is how they met *again.*

At the engagement party his friends asked, "Now where were you headed, when you bumped into her?" and he cleared his throat—for nerves, for time—and said, "Trouble," and everyone laughed.

At the wedding his brother interrupted his own toast to bend at an inebriated angle and ask, "And what was on Kennedy Boulevard anyway, that you were wandering alone, middle of Kennedy?" and he replied, from the chest, which was good because sonority and authority are often confused, and only the one fool had a microphone, "Searching high and low for this woman," and everyone applauded.

On the trip to celebrate their twenty-fifth anniversary—the four of them in Portland, Maine, after arriving on three planes and meeting at baggage claim, the destination a shrewd compromise between quaintness and nonstop service, the restaurant aboard a docked ship in the harbor, the reservation for half past five because their daughter is certain her parents are ancient—their son asks idly, as if scratching an itch, "A random day, a random sidewalk, what were the chances?" and his father replies, with the kind of compressed grin that twenty years earlier meant, *Get that hair on your head ready for tousling,* "At least as low, it turns out, as you being born."

She allows herself to look at her husband as he fights for the check. This is the man whose devotion she has admired for so long, and disliked herself for it, because isn't devotion her due? This is the man who has given her so many moments, and yet so few moments to mourn, his failures so small, relative to a quarter century, *a quarter of a century*, that they are absurd: when, during their honeymoon, on a hike through wooded hills, he found a feather with a quill as thick as a pinky and moved too quickly to show her and managed to put it in her eye, and on hearing her cry out, and before saying anything else, and without having so much as touched her, said, like a child, "But I didn't mean to"; when his friend, over at the house with his wife to watch the Super Bowl, during one of many commercials, which this gentleman misunderstood to be occasions for jabber rather than kind of the point, and after she indicated, charitably, a tiny chip-shaped piece of chip perched on his cheek, told her, very distinctly, "That's funny coming from the girl with an ass full of birthmarks," which was all the more galling because he and her husband were as close as friends could be when the only things they shared were visits to the home improvement store using the contractors' entrance though they weren't contractors and, it appeared, profoundly inappropriate information; when she opened his calendar and found, for later the same day, a dash with "Spend time" on one side and her name on the other, the line scrawled across the bottom of the appointment at 4:00 P.M. cruel for its breezy carelessness, the ending finial cruel for its hint of anticipation, the name there like it was from an almanac.

It is no use. Metal beats paper. He lets go of the check, careful to smile. He is after as kingly a surrender as possible.

As they leave the restaurant he jokes about the lunch rush, because defaming the early hour will persuade others and himself that he is not so ancient. He holds the door for her, gestures with a soft-bladed hand, inclined modestly, not flat.

Her children are not children anymore. There is more than a little proof: they have their father's height; they have cards forged from a metal no alchemist would have known to associate with five-digit credit lines. As always, though, it is the random thing that births an epiphany. The young do not revel in routeless walks, and yet here are her children proposing a stroll.

The four of them walk along the harbor. It is summer, and so the sun is in no rush, and so there are still blues enough to make a person grateful.

In twenty-five years he has never lied about it. How simple would it have been for him to say it was his future wife he'd seen from the bus, whereupon he demanded to get off because the rest of his life depended on it? That the hiss of that bus kneeling curbside was the sound of giddy windfall because he knew he had only to jog a sidewalk to claim the love of his life? So simple that most men, innocently and without calculation, would have come to remember it as what actually happened. They wouldn't need decades. Instantly they would have promoted it to memory, encouraged by its logic, rewarded by its expediency. A beautiful story in a carrying case.

This harbor reminds her of another. Except that harbor faced west, not east. One might argue a westward orientation is superior. One might argue a setting sun should flame over water, not hang above indifferent business like a bulb in a vending machine.

She knows she owes everything to another woman. The notion is preposterous, maybe delusional. She will not be the self-dramatizing suburbanite, grasping for grievances and contriving jealousies. She will not debase all they've built together by monumentalizing a name she knows nothing about. Possibly it was a slip of the tongue. Certainly it means nothing against all they've lived since. On the other hand, she remembers his eyes. She remembers how a man without a word of Spanish knew to pronounce it the way he did.

But it is irrelevant. Years ago she convinced herself it was irrelevant. And after two glasses of wine it is central. Her life was born of a moment, and the mother of that moment was a stranger after her husband. She found true love by mistake. This life is a hand-me-down.

They walk in pairs, father and son ahead, mother and daughter behind. The men talk across a ledge of shoulder. Together they mull an expanse of twenty-five years, father gesturing matter-of-factly and son disbelieving, contrary to evidence, that this expanse will one day be his, also the matched pair of grousing knees. The women talk under bowed heads. The scant air between them has the shape of contentment. They pace off the same territory as the men, but more efficiently, because they laugh at the sharpest truths rather than go wide around them.

Her son is a carbon-based copy of her husband—the same eagerness to please strangers, the same embrace of hard work so intense that accomplishments bring unease and even depression for ending what came before, the same talent for hiding emotion and, the brilliant twist, exuding the pleasantest vanilla cheerfulness to deter others from sensing something amiss, from hunting for more. They could be fuming mad, those two, and to look at them you'd swear they were thinking about clouds and cream horns.

But the motive for concealment is almost always its vulnerability. Hunting blinds are a challenge because of all that rifle; stoicism works until your eyes want to know if it's working. By the time her son was old enough to deploy his talent, it was over. It was done. She had had years with his father to learn what to look for, and the moment she saw that dimming in the eyes, like ten minutes to closing and the next room goes dark, she knew. It got to the point where she could detect the slightest flicker. And she had years to perfect countermeasures—digging deeper on subjects they seemed positively glad about, or looking away when asking questions because this made them curious whether she really cared, and that meant they peered harder and divulged more as they answered.

Which is how somewhere between baggage claim and the hotel she knew her son's roommate was not a roommate. Which is how sometime between appetizers and entrées she knew to wonder how many monthly payments on that glinting credit card he'd missed.

She knows another thing. With that daughter of hers, so prudent and down-to-earth, giving her mother so little to worry about, she allows herself too much. She finds herself confiding in her, as she would in a friend. She sees her daughter's plate clean of problems and fills it with rumors of others. It's an old habit. When Katie was young, she doled out too much information about acquaintances, even about the mothers of Katie's classmates. She knew the mistake in this, and once gave herself a rule that only if her daughter asked a question would she allow herself to speak to matters that fairly bore on it. Another mistake. The ring around this rule expanded under the heat of banter, enough to admit everything.

She does not remember how many times they've talked about it. Really she does not remember talking about it at all. She knows only that the family record—every family has one, accreting bit by bit with information so curt and desultory and incidental, heard through a sweater being pulled over a head, dispensed as the good dressing is retrieved from the fridge, that there should be no room for mendacity, no time for invention, and the cumulative result seems solid and un-impeachable as a reef—the family record has it that she was reunited with her true love after she moved back to town, and that she moved back to town because she'd had enough, and that she'd had enough because she was ready again for warmth and familiarity after a city that could stay so cold even in summer, even with the exertions of millions straining to prove themselves.

Love promises fairy tales. Life delivers waiting and tissue paper with anxious shapes torn from the corners and hugs that feel from the neck up like cold cuts.

In truth, she came back to get rid of the apartment she'd subleased. She needed to empty the storage locker and check the particleboard drawers for anything identifying before she paid the leering guy at the front desk entirely too much to take the contents to the nearest Dumpster. She came back to say good-bye to a couple of girlfriends. And to board a plane.

Is she the liar? For never having told. The omission grew each time she let her husband think he was the duplicitous one. And now, decades later, it made sense. Who would suspect secrets so tirelessly, who would gouge with her own eyes the eyes of others, but a person who knew from secrets?

She tells Katie almost everything.

She has allowed herself to imagine the conversation. Not often. But more than once.

Do not ask me what was on Kennedy Boulevard, she'd say.

Wait, what?

From a young age her daughter would have understood the reference. Kennedy Boulevard was part of the family record, celebrated by aunts and uncles who were bankers and upholsterers and not a bard bone in their bodies, yet who reveled in the story, told it as all good stories are told—with the proper amount of tension in the jaw, to signal, *This is treasure not often let out of this mouth*, to signal, *You really should take a hint from this rigid jaw and brace yourself*—for what they considered its lesson that so much can come from so little.

I said, Do not ask me what was on Kennedy Boulevard.

What was on Kennedy Boulevard?

During her second pregnancy, when it came time to pick a name, it was like choosing where in open desert to pitch camp for the night. They knew it would be a girl. That did not help a lot. Her mother had a passable name, but hated it, and strictly forbade them from compounding the mistake. His mother had a Greek name, from the myths, but—this is the reason she gave her husband—there wasn't a single Greek in the family tree.

She had her own ideas. She was careful to build up to it. She had one chance to watch for his reaction. One chance to finally know.

"Julie?"

"Julie's the girl everyone likes but no one remembers," he said.

"What about—"

"Will there be a woman president?" he went on. "Sure. Mark my words, there will never be a president named Julie."

"I will. I will mark them ridiculous. Katherine."

"Maybe. Everyone will call her Kathy. Kathy or Kate. We have to be OK with that."

She was sure to fix her eyes on his before she started pronouncing.

"Alicia?"

Four syllables.

He considered.

"Yeah, I don't hate it," he said finally, "but I don't love it, either."

Left eye, nothing. Right eye. Nothing.

"What else you got?" he said.

Left eye again. Nothing.

"Nothing," she said.

And to her daughter she'd reply, in the singsong tones one saves for stories with no sequels, *On Kennedy Boulevard, there was a travel agency that held an airline ticket to Crete and a fiancé who waited there.*

Never has she told anyone. Why should she? It is the man who commands admiration for opportunity costs, who chooses bravely from multiple lives competing for his favor. The sacrifice for love is the man's story. The woman, meanwhile, awaits rescue, but no villain, no dragon to justify a triumphant entrance, no discernible risk to the hero at all, really, his friends egging him on to hear the story again even though he vanquished nothing: just a damsel in this dress.

She has told Katie too many things, but never that.

What would have been the lesson? That you fly and you fly and you do not stop when the world taps you on the shoulder? That, no, you live relentlully, that you go ready to pause and turn at every new circumstance because she has it on good authority that each time the very best things in life may be waiting?

She is in no position to teach lessons. In the end, she knows so little. What she remembers from that sidewalk is a man cowed by his error. What she in fact saw, without knowing it, was a man bewildered—vanquished, in fact—on recognizing the look on her face: the look of someone finding something and never wanting to lose it again.

Certain memories, flawless, do not improve with chatter. He has never spoken of it.

How? How is it she does not understand the moment at the heart of her life?

There is more than one reason. Because her eyes lacked practice and gave up more than they took in. Because divining the truth about others forgets how much of others we are.

Because this is the part about fate.

They stop in front of the hotel. The kids make to go inside. They are careful to mention the possibility they might go out again. It is obvious to everyone they will, that of course they'll go up and change clothes and spray smells on themselves and light out into the evening. And yet here they are, her grown son and daughter, sheepish like preteens, and unsure, as if embarrassed for not asking permission.

Their parents pretend not to notice. They kiss these kids good night as a bus rumbles by. They hug these giants who already smell perfect. It feels like everything good in its proper place.

They let them go and set out again, back toward the water. Away from the sun, which sinks behind cornice and bulk. Nothing kingly about this surrender–quite the opposite. This sun is humble to the end, unfurling from behind a carpet of velvet gray everywhere they go.

When he extends his hand, she takes it, happily. She leans on it as she takes a first step, brings it to her side for the second, and the third, and ever after.

THE GIRL WHO NOT
ONCE CRIED WOLF

For Claire Kane Choundas

THERE ARE NO GERMAN SHOPS IN BLITZENSTOCK, GERMANY. Only shops.

On hiring a coach at Pflanze's Inn, you do not direct the driver to Heiborgplatz Castle. It is the only castle near Blitzenstock. You simply say, "The castle." Or maybe, "The castle, please," if it is Sunday and good feeling abounds. Otherwise the coachman will fix you for an arrogant city-dweller, turn in his seat just far enough to publish his disdain, and— still presenting the side of his face, and so letting you think you'll remain at rest for moments longer—launch the horses abruptly from that very portrait position and rock you into the back rail like an unloved package.

Not far from the castle, across the Hügelbezirk River, is the Blue Wood of Brunnen. Some say every tree there has a half-moon mark somewhere on its trunk—you just have to find it—while others say every tree in the world has a half-moon mark somewhere and you find what you want to. In any event, no one calls it the Blue Wood of Brunnen. Except Wilhelm, the magistrate's son, but Wilhelm is strange and instead of greeting people just whispers their names absently and audibly, over and over, as if thinking privately but not so secretly about them; and likes to go to school with the sash that hangs from his cap tucked into the back of his shirt after having tired of the older boys yanking back on it and wiping their noses with it and tying it to the inside doorknob of the girls' bathroom in the church hall because he is too sheepish to trespass himself and untie it, or even to abandon the cap altogether, and instead waits abjectly for the girls to discover and unleash him; and has an older, green-eyed brother named Jacob who cants back when he walks like he doesn't care about anything but in fact is quite studious and the only time he spoke to Riding Hood told her she had a face like a skylark.

Everyone except Wilhelm calls it simply "the woods."

Which is why, contrary to belief, the moment of revelation for Riding Hood did not come when she remarked the size of the wolf's teeth. Nor when she heard the wolf retort, "All the better to eat you all up!" in less a growl than a detonation. The moment of revelation, of horrific revelation, came much earlier:

"Who is it?" (A hoarse voice. Like a millstone dragged across a courtyard. Not at all Grandma's normal voice. But Grandma was sick. Mother said very sick. Of course she was hoarse.)

"Grandma, it's me."

"Come in, come in."

(Opened the door. Closed it behind her. Saw a rumpled sleeping cap and rioting tufts of hair. Didn't need more to know Grandma looked terrible.)

"Hello, Grandma."

"Hello, *Little Red Riding Hood*."

This. This was the moment.

Never in twelve years had her grandmother called her "Little Red Riding Hood." She was Riding Hood. Always had been. To friends and family, to everyone except those to whom she was being introduced for the first time. (And except her new violin teacher, who even after four lessons called her Little Red Riding Hood, but maybe with time would call her "Riding Hood" instead, and maybe wouldn't, because Frau Lehrer, with her lustrous coiffure and exquisite intellect, could not be predicted.)

That thing in the bed knew her name from overhearing it somewhere.

That thing in the bed was not Grandma.

Why, then, did what followed follow? Why did Riding Hood waste valuable time? Why did she marvel with a methodical naiveté at all the ways this wolf did not resemble her grandmother, if already she knew the truth?

Do not be misled. Naiveté had nothing to do with it. This was cool calculation. Most versions of the story omit Riding Hood's exceeding self-possession. But I won't. She needed time to think. And she found a way to get it.

Most versions nowhere record that, as large as the wolf's eyes really were, Riding Hood opened hers even wider, because the clever know how to look fatuous, and the brave do not mind seeming pitiable.

"*My*, Grandma," the girl ventured, "what big eyes you have."

Riding Hood roved her eyes this way and that. The wolf thought she was just being silly, showing how big she thought his eyes looked. But this roving of the eyes was camouflage. It was pretext to use those eyes to reconnoiter the house, to scrutinize every corner. Riding Hood counted (correctly) on the wolf being too dismissive to notice.

Observations: The closet and bathroom doors stood open. Grandma was nowhere in the house.

Deduction: Grandma would never tolerate a single door left ajar—let alone leave the house with two doors wide open. Thus Grandma had never left the house.

Hypothesis: Grandma was inside the wolf's belly.

"The better to see you with, my dear," said the wolf.

Still in bed, the wolf propped himself up and yawned and locked shining eyes on Riding Hood. Grandma's spectacles sat so tiny on his brutal snout they looked like a second, filmier pair of nostrils. The head was just massive. As it lifted, bed sheets poured from it like rapids off a boulder, revealing neck and shoulders and chest. He was wearing Grandma's nightgown. The fabric strained against his bulk. But where Grandma would have offered a round bosom, there was only a flat mass, like a pile of planking. Suddenly Riding Hood thrilled with glorious indignation—hot and potent and ridiculous—because in the way of bosoms this wolf, however fearsome, was hopelessly outmatched.

This small exultation steeled her. Quick, did she have something, anything, she could use for a weapon?

No. She had a basket. That's it. A basket and a spice cake wrapped in a checkered gingham handkerchief.

Weapons? Please. She was thinking like a boy. She needed to stop that. She needed to find out whether Grandma was still alive. Nothing else mattered.

It occurred to her that Grandma might be shouting for help at that very moment. Would she hear a voice coming from inside the wolf? She needed a sustained quiet, entirely pure of any talk, so she could strain for the slightest sound.

"*My*, Grandma," said Riding Hood, "what big ears you have."

Riding Hood trained her eyes on one of the wolf's ears and shifted her face through an intricacy of expressions—first merely distracted, then curious, followed by amused, inquiring, disturbed, scandalized, admiring, awed, now curious again—one after another, at just the right speed, because too slow would invite interruption, and too fast would fail to transfix. The wolf sat riveted, watching the show. All the while Riding Hood listened.

It was no use. All she heard was the wolf's breathing, a racket like wind through the kind of worthless twiggery that little girls might gather and that their fathers stand well within their rights to snort at but instead pile cheerfully alongside the firewood to make their daughters feel useful and valiant.

Riding Hood understood with a lash of shame that she was being absurd. The point was to play the fool, not *be* the fool. That body was so big, the fur so coarse. There was no hope she would hear anyone in there, let alone her frail, flute-throated grandmother.

Riding Hood had to go in there herself. She had to get right inside the wolf's belly to see if Grandma was all right. But how would she get past that mouth and its battery of knives? If her grandmother was still alive, it was because she'd been swallowed whole. This wolf was certainly huge enough to have gulped her down. But he had too many teeth for her to believe this was likely. She had seen them when he yawned. She had tried to ignore them when he yawned. But how do you ignore teeth like crags, teeth like lancets, narwhal tusks, scramasaxes, cathedral spires, petiolar stipules, teeth like triple-spaded bayonets?

Two of the teeth had their own teeth.

Even if he'd swallowed her whole, what were the chances he'd do it again? Maybe it was a habit, maybe he always gulped his food entire. Or maybe he did that only when ravenous, but now—partly sated—he'd take his time and let his teeth enjoy themselves.

"The better to hear you with, my dear."

Riding Hood's heart jumped. The wolf's voice had changed. It was flat, utterly free of inflection. It had the tone of wanting to get things over with.

She had to dive clean into that mouth. She had to plunge down the throat and—once she felt the gut open up around her—tuck under and find the bottom of the wolf's belly with her buttocks.

But she needed to time it perfectly. She needed to launch herself into that mouth just after the teeth parted and before they closed again. If only she could know in advance how and when those teeth would open and shut.

But then—her heart racing and her head a cauldron of blood—she realized she *did* know.

She gaped her eyes wider than ever, telegraphing a flattering terror, and cried out, "*My*, Grandma, what big teeth you have!"

And the wolf stretched back his lips, and Riding Hood discovered she didn't know the half of it, because he had molars like scythes and maces and falchions she had not glimpsed before, and the wolf—avid to fill his mouth with this chirping treat who smelled of spice cake, eager to sop up the building drool with this cape that wrapped so lasciviously, with this hood already stained the proper color so the deed was halfway done—bellowed, "The better to eat you with!"

Which is when Riding Hood leaped into the brute's steaming mouth.

To be specific, it was during that pair of moments between the "t" in "eat" and the "th" in "with" that Riding Hood dove in. She had correctly guessed what the wolf would say. And so she timed her vault accordingly. "T" and "th" were sounds that sealed off the mouth. Between those sounds glittered her two-moment window of opportunity.

The first moment swelled voluptuously with the word "you." This wolf favored the acid taste of horror in his prey, and so he drew out the word longer than necessary.

The second moment was complicated by the "w" in "with." Lips not quite closed but threatening, black like a hound's and prehensile like a devil's, coiling oozing snakes awakened in their nest, grasping at her waist in mid-dive, but all the better: they did not stop her progress, and in fact pointed her like a barrel around a bullet into the hole of the throat. She did not know it, but without their lucky intervention, she was destined to die—to carom against the palate and meet with her soft parts the spikes and spines that hid alongside the molars like a secret squadron.

It was so black where she landed it took time to convince herself she was no longer moving. There was a horrific stench. She got up. For the first time she felt helpless—not for the reason you'd think, not because she'd found herself inside a wolf's stomach—but because every time she took a step, the floor sagged and drifted and quivered. There was no good place to stand. How long could a person last in a place where even standing still was precarious?

With time the darkness released. She started to see things: wrack and ruin and all of it slick and bubbling with a layer like congealed sweat. She recognized her grandmother's writing desk. Or pieces of it, rather. The pieces were large enough that the striped inlay, black walnut and brown chestnut, was still discernible. The pieces were heaped up against what looked like a wall made of tongue. A pool of slime lapped at the base of the pile.

As Riding Hood moved, she felt prickings against her legs and hips. Like from burrs and thorns, except these things were larger, more substantial. She stumbled over something long and thin.

It was not a branch.

Riding Hood was inside a forest of undigested bones.

And then she saw her grandmother. She was half sitting—Riding Hood could not make out what on or against—and half lying down. Her head hung back too far. It was a reckless angle that suggested worse than sleep. Riding Hood set the basket down. She removed the gingham handkerchief from the basket, took off her hooded cape, and made her way to her grandmother. Shuffling. Because stepping would only tempt some pronging hardness. Even before

Riding Hood got close enough to see the gash across her grandmother's forehead, she had decided. Cape in left hand, handkerchief in right, she made up her mind.

If her grandmother was dead, she'd find some way to climb to the ceiling. She'd thrust the cape into the wolf's throat, from below, and choke him to death. She would die, she and her grandmother would both be dead, and that was fine, because this monster would never hurt anyone again.

If her grandmother was alive, she'd use the handkerchief, not the cape. Tickling his throat would cause the wolf to rasp and cough, maybe. The thunderstorm of noise would bring help. Maybe.

Riding Hood took her grandmother's hand. Grandma stirred, opened her eyes finally.

"Riding Hood . . ." is all Grandma said. No sweetness to these sounds, no surprise. Her eyes closed again. The words were grim, and final, as if seeing Riding Hood there had killed her last hope.

Riding Hood did not want to talk. Grown-ups think they know even when they don't, and Riding Hood knew exactly what to do and Grandma didn't, and so Riding Hood did not want to talk. She wanted to hurry. She bent over and kissed Grandma firmly on the forehead, like a grown-up who knew. Only when Riding Hood found herself swaying atop a pile of refuse, readying her handkerchief, did it occur to her she had kissed an open wound.

Which is how a girl with a clot of blood on her lips, and from it the taste of old armor in her mouth, came to be the first conqueror ever to plant a flag up instead of down.

Inches above Riding Hood's head was a hive of red flesh. It was the gullet, but it resembled more an infestation than any organ: hairy webs of crimson, knotted and gobby and dripping, braided into a single undulating mass. She couldn't find a hole. It was galling to think she could not find the thing through which she had traveled just minutes earlier. This goaded her into looking harder, and less from any good deduction than this spasm of irritated will did she conclude that the spot near the center, the one more obviously inflamed and gleaming than any surrounding membrane, with a convexity that seemed opposite to the hole she was looking for, was where the throat ended.

She used a corner of the handkerchief. She raked it across this angry blood-filled egg. Nothing.

She folded the corner for two-ply stiffness and tried again. Nothing.

"Oh, be careful," bleated her grandmother from below. She said this without looking up.

Riding Hood made a fist and bunched the handkerchief around it and let it fly, again and again. She punished whatever she could reach, pounding at the main protuberance and for good measure all its suppurating suburbs.

Of course, her grandmother wasn't looking up. She didn't have her spectacles, she couldn't see. Why would she be looking up? That was why she wasn't looking up.

Smiting and smashing with that veiled fist and still nothing. Riding Hood bent to pick up a bristling wedge of wood, the narrow end more ragged than pointy. She had not yet straightened up when she felt under her feet a violent shaking. Then she heard it: a distant rumbling, louder now, closer by the moment, headed straight for her. Whatever it was, it was com—

An explosion.

Slammed up against the ceiling, scraped across it, around her a roar like ten oceans, white blurs of flying bone, barbs of wood and twists of metal bulleting everywhere, biting into her face, needling into her arms, everything a porridge of bone dust and rancid sweat, shards and splints of bone sailing in sheets like rain in a windstorm, flung down to the floor so hard she could not conceive of breathing, a booming screeching roaring like the world and its twenty oceans breaking in half, launched back up, up, even more terrifying than getting crushed against the ceiling, no ceiling at all, nothing to stop this, nothing to stop her, soaring and soaring up and endlessly.

Riding Hood had miscalculated. She'd wanted a thunderstorm. She'd caused an earthquake. The wolf had vomited.

She landed in the middle of the room, bounced once, and skidded across the floor into the front door. Her grandmother dropped in a loose pile alongside her, facedown. Seeing this infuriated Riding Hood and, though the stun of her fall had replaced her lungs with a pair of agonies and her hearing with a soundless shimmering, she charged straight at the wolf.

She lunged with her right hand, less quickly than she was capable of. She let the wolf snap around and down and catch her in a maw so massive that rather than shred her arm he impaled it with a single fang. The wolf, finally tasting blood, roved his eyes this way and that. The right teared up in ecstasy and the left surveyed her face, greedy to consume the slightest fear and pain visible there, but stayed hungry. Neither saw her left hand coming. She swung it in a wild arc. The wedge of wood it held—the one she'd found in the wolf's belly and in her panic never put down—dug so far into the happy eye that the lid could have closed over it nicely: a rolltop on a writing desk.

The wolf squealed and bolted through the front door just as it opened from the outside. It was a stranger who opened it. Passing through the woods this hunter had heard a far-off and improbably loud noise. A rockfall? Approaching the cottage, he'd seen no signs of danger, but proceeded cautiously. For his trouble he got a nasty cut on the cheek and two broken ribs as the wolf rammed past.

The hunter helped Riding Hood rouse Grandma, who was shaken and bruised but, forehead aside, uninjured. Riding Hood looked terrible. She'd been at the apex of the stomach, and so everything in it, throatbound, had headed straight for her like a magnet. Her face and hands were lattices of cuts and scratches. Riding Hood immediately told the hunter everything that had happened, not to console herself (though she was sure he suspected this was why), but to stop the grown-ups from making such a fuss. Also, she sensed the hunter's embarrassment for having failed so instantly to be of help, and thought maybe this reportage would restore his sense of authority. The hunter said "It was nothing" as Riding Hood dabbed at his wound, a pulpy thing in the shape of a half-moon, and "It is nothing" when Riding Hood insisted that he hold the handkerchief there and take it with him.

These were the same phrases he repeated in the weeks thereafter. In the weeks thereafter the hunter carried with him the handkerchief and dandled it conspicuously (and in mixed company never managed to put it away) and contrived every opportunity to tell the girl's tale, the one she'd told while holding the handkerchief to his face, but now casting himself as the hero, and at the end narrating a just and dashing slaughter in place of an escape. "It was nothing," he'd intone, again and again, sometimes for the admiration that modesty brings, sometimes for shelter from the detailed questions that admiration brings, and never did that charlatan make a truer statement, because his account was such a heap of fictive trash, further contaminated with each retelling as it spread from town to town through a tavern-addled network of exactly those miscreants least concerned with or capable of the truth, that "nothing" is the best word for it.

I know, because I heard him tell the story once—for the last time, in fact—on the side of a road, when he was swollen and tangy with drink.

Riding Hood shared her story with a few others.

She told her grandmother, because she was unconscious for nearly all the good parts. Over tea and strudel, because after their adventure neither could abide the reek of spice cake. And the scars on Grandma's forehead and Riding Hood's forearm didn't match perfectly, but they liked to pretend they did, because the clever know how much of life must be imagined, and the brave do not mind seeming frivolous.

She told her mother, of course. And her mother held her tight, and told her how proud her father would have been, and finally to stop all the tears said, "*My*, Riding Hood, what strong arms you have." And Riding Hood could not really reply. All the better to fight for the ones she loved, is what she was thinking, what she would have said. But there was no plausible way to say it, because no one calls the ones they love the ones they love. They are simply the ones. The only ones. They are simply all that matters.

And she told me. During our very first lesson. You have the story here just as she recounted it. Getting her to tell it was easy. The young ones believe if they push up their sleeves to the elbows, they'll play like Pisendel. I saw her scar in the fifth minute of the lesson and a fantastic sweetness trickled down my throat.

I teeter on hind legs, and the mothers ask me if they're too old to also take lessons. I don a wig and a frock and an ensorcelling double-extract of violet, and the fathers dart glances and wonder if they'd like a different sort of lesson. I keep a prim mouth around my vowels for teeth's sake, and none of these dolts have the slightest suspicion. The girl did her polite best to ignore the fustian patch and confide in the good eye. She told me plenty. About her adventure; about her friend Wilhelm (who, what are the chances, is the same Wilhelm as my pupil Wilhelm, an awkward youngster, sent by his magistrate father for lessons, with no sense of pitch and a limited intellect and the habit of absently whispering "Dog, dog" for no reason); about how I was wrong about fermatas, insisting as much no matter how hard I glared through my giant monocle, because fermatas did not merely extend a note for roughly half again its length but rather licensed a player to hold it for "as long as she might please"; about how she wanted to be a scientist, like her father had been.

This is a girl who never called for help, who not once showed fear. A girl like this is not easily forgotten. A temptation like this is not easily abjured.

Why, then, do I bide my time? Why do I let lesson after lesson float past and allow myself only the smell of her buttery body? Why do I still call her "Little Red Riding Hood"?

Because I want to hear every detail, every last tiny new one that layers in with each telling. Because no small part of the savor of a meal is the anticipation. And because I want her to feel—just before the keening agony of these teeth introduced, one by one, into her tender organs—the hot spike of regret, of self-blame, just as I have, for every opportunity she had and still lost.

I swear it, on little Wilhelm's stupidity I swear it.

She will never live to know what it means to have a face like a skylark.

YOU WILL EXCUSE ME

He washes his hands. He has shaken a lot of them.

He dries his hands. The backs of them, too.

Really he takes his time washing to put off what follows. He knows this but does it anyway.

Each time the restroom door opens, the sounds rush in. A broad and liquid hum, cocktail glasses, a woman laughing. Bells floating on ocean.

When he goes, he does not have to wait. Immediately it runs red.

It used to be a flecking. A light intermittent pinking. The first time, it was a flecking for a long while before it ran red. Back when it was a mere concern, a curiosity even. A dashboard threatening to peel. A neighbor's porch with one newspaper too many.

Now, in the mornings, sometimes it is still a flecking. Maybe that is not true.

When he was young, he liked to roil every part of the surface. The stream made continents of foam when passed over clear water. Passed over these continents, the same stream destroyed them.

Last time it did not go so quickly to red, last time. Before he understood it was something.

One adulthood and how many mailing addresses later and he had forgotten about continents. No room between conference calls for continents.

In the mornings it is more than a flecking, a very generous flecking, but still. It has not entirely turned color, after all. It is not as bad as that.

When they told him it had come back, he did not show surprise, did not act like much.

A frizzy sensation at the tip now. Nothing to do with pathology. Just physics. A garden hose at full force, put to the skin, will astonish with how much of a thing, mere material, subject to other things, a person is.

She was at the kitchen table with her glasses on. He was proud of how calmly he told her. His eyes were calm gleams in his face, he made sure of that.

The first time it was a young doctor, vibrating with chatter and optimism. This second one is older. This second one breathes through his nose, slowly, deliberately. He can hear this man breathe against himself when he looks down to write things. Battle-hardened, for a hard battle, for hardly a battle.

When strafed, the continents actually bleed now. No game in that.

At least the doctor did not smile when he said it. Doctors

that old can say what they like. "The only guarantee," this one said, "is there are no guarantees."

Briefly, briefly, but he saw it, she looked at the back of her hand after he told her, she looked there before she looked up at him, the same hand she favors to muss his hair and muss it back, the hand that gripped his ear in a light twist as they came out of their first kiss and her saying, "Now remember that when it's time to call me," that tap-tapped the other when he produced the ring but forgot to put it on, that he grasped while she squatted otherwise unassisted over a bedpan after the epidural ("Never seen that in twenty years," said the nurse, "and I been doing this twenty years"), that he held at his brother's funeral and put over his eyes like a blindfold as he bent away from her so she could not see and of course she saw. Before she looked back up at him.

The same stream. It destroys because it's the second time around.

Had that old doctor smiled while saying it, he might have smashed in that sagging mouth.

He does not remember it going to red so quickly. The time before.

He washes his hands. He dries his hands. The backs of them, too.

He knows it but he does it anyway. Really he takes his time washing to put off what follows.

The restroom door opens. He goes back to the people, those sounds, these faces, and pretends there are good things in store.

ON THE FAR SIDE OF THE SEA

A MAN SO RICH, SO YOUNG, LEARNS TO EXPECT FAVOR. YOUTH TELLS him the world is an eager thing. Wealth says it holds presents.

The dog Basil had two purposes: to scent quarry, and to unspoil his master of these expectations. Because everything about this dog was a trial.

This time it was a flaking door. A brown flaking door that once was red. The dog Basil was now scratching at it. A hovel in the middle of a humid wood with a brown flaking door. What this dog hunted was mischief.

Just as the man and his manservant caught up, just as both bent to wrench him up by that scruff, the door opened. The men straightened. In the doorway stood a woman.

"Which one of you hates my door?" She said this to the dog.

They looked at her. She was a different woman. She

made her own light. Or parts of her did. Her eyes flashed, and her teeth gleamed, and off her hair danced coins and flosses of shine. The man forgot to say something.

"Silence all around," she said. "A genuine mystery." Finally she looked up at the man.

"My dog," he managed to say. The butt of his long gun was resting on the ground. He dragged it forward as if this helped explain. "Apologies for my dog."

The woman put a white finger on the barrel of the gun and pushed. When it leaned quite away, she removed the finger. Without retracting it, she leveled it at the dog.

"You and your masters and their apologies should come in and have something hot."

Indoors it smelled like mountainside. There was only one room. Surprisingly it felt spacious. Or perhaps just sparse. The only things were the chairs they sat on, a bed and a hearth, a yellow stove, a kidney-shaped mirror.

And books. Many appeared to be music books, but nowhere was there an instrument.

They had something hot. None of the cups matched.

"Haven't had many visitors since my mother passed," she said. The words suggested apology, the tone none at all. "I may have gotten used to the solitude."

She stood to refill the manservant's cup.

"No offense to present company," she added quickly, sitting down again. "I do enjoy the occasional guest. Even the kind that stares."

The man looked stricken. "I am so sorry," he said.

"I was speaking of the dog." She cleared her throat. "What is his name?"

The question was charity, to cut short his embarrassment. He was grateful.

"Basil," he said. "After the herb. He's a scent hound."

"A dog named after a food. Two of my favorite things."

"What about trouble? Because that is this dog's favorite thing."

The dog raised his chin off his paws and, using the corners of his eyes for each of them in turn, gave a yelp.

On their way out, the man could think of nothing clever, and simply asked the woman her name. She told him and asked his. The manservant picked up both guns. They had left them outside. When after a few steps the man looked back, she was still at the doorway. Her mouth seemed to be moving still, as if repeating his name.

Two days later, the man returned. This time he came alone. The door still flaked. A green blade of something fernish wandered across the lower half. It looked to him like a dog turnstile. This amused him until it dismayed him. He was having frivolous thoughts just when he could not afford to feel frivolous.

The door opened.

"You," she said.

"And you," he said.

It was awkward at first. The way he kept his head down reminded her of a burglar. The way she kept her arms crossed made him feel petty for thinking it made her seem haughty.

But it was easier without the yelping.

He drank from the same cup she'd used during his first visit. She noticed this with some embarrassment on handing it to him. He noticed the cup, and the embarrassment, and, pleased to spare her more, that his left-handed grip would keep his mouth from where she'd placed hers.

Both of them pretended not to notice how long they'd been talking. Partly they were enjoying things. Partly they did not want to ruin the small delight of announcing surprise at how much time had passed.

When that moment came and went, and it was time to leave, he could think of nothing clever. He told her where he lived, because that was where he was going. Instantly he was sorry, because he lived in a castle, and it sounded pompous. She only nodded her head.

He returned the next day. But no one answered.

He knocked again. Nothing.

He waited what he thought a handful of grown men would agree was time enough for a reasonable nap, in case she was taking one. Then he knocked again.

He waited for hours. He had given his staff the day off. He was in no hurry to return home.

He worried. Maybe she'd left. Maybe she'd tired of her solitary life and found an appealing cliff. Maybe she was inside, determined not to subject herself again to what surely she remembered as the monotony of their last encounter.

Maybe she'd left forever.

He returned the next day. He had not finished knocking when the door moved.

"You," she said.

"No," he said. "You."

***

It was late afternoon. Outside the light fell fat and careless through the trees. Like their other late afternoon conversations—they'd had weeks of them—this one roamed.

The way she had of folding her arms against herself made him feel something between urgency and not getting air.

The way he kept his head bowed but flickered his eyes up at her at the ends of sentences left the back of her neck damp.

They were talking music, and how she'd played the harpsichord as a child ("I've told you that before, forgive me." "No, I don't think so."), and how the truest compliments were always the least graciously received, and about the forest outside.

"You'll never get lost if you remember moss grows to the north," he said.

"Or if I stay indoors while remembering it," she said.

Then about how things seemed more significant when they took place in raw nature: words, revelations, stories. She thought of Orpheus among the rocks and trees. He recalled Jesus in the desert.

"Jesus?" she repeated.

"Yes, Jesus."

She shifted in her chair.

"Did I say something wrong?" he asked.

"No, no," she said, the second unpersuasive as the first. She was examining her wrist with her fingers, but roughly, like she'd discovered a weak pulse and there was nothing for it.

"I suppose I've never been too religious," she said.

"What is too religious?"

He meant this earnestly. She thought he was being clever.

"Thinking you will get an answer," she said, "when for years you watch someone suffer and ask why."

He realized she'd misunderstood. He kept this to himself.

"Because I got no answer," she continued. "Which did not make it any easier. Or her suffering any more meaningful." She had not let go of her wrist.

"I'm sorry," he said, and very quietly, because he believed strong women like this were generally on prickly relations with sympathy.

Abruptly, as if she hadn't heard him—indeed, almost interrupting him—she said, "What appeals to you about it?"

"What?"

"Your faith. Him. The miracles, I suppose? Turning loaves to fishes?"

"Loaves to—You do know he raised someone from the dead?"

"I do," she said. "I also know he said, 'Turn the other cheek,' and then beat up the moneychangers."

"Well—"

"Bit of a hypocrite, wasn't he?"

"Sacrilege!" But he said it smiling.

"Also incompetent. Supposedly divine, but couldn't stop one of his own disciples from getting him killed. For a bag of change."

"I wouldn't put it that way." The smile was gone.

"Silver, then," she said. "And hardly a secret, mind, because the prophets had been predicting it for centuries. Allegedly."

His chin came down an inch: the aborted nod of someone concluding something.

"And his faithlessness?" he asked.

"What?"

"You've forgotten about the cross. 'My God, my God, why have you forsaken me?' While dying on the cross."

"Exactly. Yes. While dying for us. Setting such a fine example."

He swallowed. It had the two-part noise of a swallow, but loud: a key in a lock, the same key turning.

"You are offensive," he said.

"That's fine. Tell me why I am *wrong*."

She sat back in her chair. It was an act of condescension and infuriating. He wondered if there was any scripture about getting comfortable in a chair in hell.

"You've missed the point entirely," he said.

She waited.

"Those aren't coincidences," he said. "He shows a lack of integrity, incompetence. No devotion at the very moment it counts. What are those?"

"What are what?"

"Virtues, three fundamental virtues. A man without those things, it does not matter who you are, what others think of you. He was flawed in exactly those ways for reasons. A reason."

He was losing his fluency. She wondered if he was getting excited. His voice was smooth, though.

"He was God," he continued, "but a man, too. He was not perfect. And those of us who are men also, imperfect also, we are not worthless or hopeless. His flaws were a reassurance. We can be good as God."

She wondered whether he had delivered this before. And on the surface of that thought formed a bead of alarm.

Maybe this was all a mistake. Maybe he was a religious fanatic, all that brown ruggish hair a trap.

"That's what I've always thought, anyway," he said. "That the flaws were—kindnesses. Invitations, gentle ones. To be better."

The fluster in this last part was a relief to hear. This was not a speech. It was the decanting of too many hours thinking alone.

"Interesting," she said.

"True," he said.

She laughed.

"Marry me," he said.

She smiled, put her hands on her knee, and waited. As if he were sharing something amusing but hadn't finished.

"What?" she said finally.

It was ridiculous. He didn't mind.

"Marry me," he said.

She did not shake her head. It was a slower motion, like rubbing first one cheek and then the other against a fur.

"Why?"

His face fell.

"I am a good man."

"I mean, why are you asking me?"

Those flashing eyes were not built to return steady looks, but he dared them anyway.

"Because you are what I want."

Each time, he made up his mind not to bring it up. Each time, it burned under his skin, as if an encampment there of jawed beetles was settling down to work, until he said it, blurting it out, and he did not know why, though somewhere in his head there was a notion he could not let history say it was he who had lost her for want of trying.

"Marry me."

"Again?"

"No, it would be the first time."

She just looked at him. In some ways they acted like they were already married.

"Marry me, please."

He had not seen her in a long while. She had forbidden him from visiting until he learned to keep his promises.

Each time, he had left promising he would not speak of marriage the next time. Each time, he had broken that promise.

This was a delicate record for a man selling a lifelong promise.

He asked his manservant to go. He knew this was absurd but asked anyway.

"What would I say?" his manservant asked.

"That I love her."

"I think she knows."

"Because I've told her," said the man.

"Right."

"Well then, maybe hearing it from someone else will make it real for her," the man said. "Objective."

The manservant considered this.

"Should I mention marriage?" he asked.

"I can't stop you," said the man, "but you should know I love another."

The manservant, not knowing to laugh, just looked at him.

The man rubbed his chin with a curled finger. "Please do."

The manservant returned that afternoon.

"She was very polite. But very firm."

"About what exactly?"

The manservant looked down and blinked several times. He was preparing what to say.

"I asked her as many different ways as I could. Short of being rude." The manservant shifted in place. "Finally she mentioned her mother. She was not entirely clear. Something about love getting in the way of life. Or yielding to life, no—life yielding to love. Or—" He stopped. "She was not entirely clear."

"Her mother?" The man leaned forward. "If she wasn't clear, how firm could she have been?"

"She doesn't want marriage. She was clear about that."

The man went "puh" with his lips. He reviewed the lower parts of the room.

"How does she look?" he asked finally. "Does she look well?"

"She does, she looks well." The manservant nibbled thoughtfully on nothing. "She does have the strangest habit. Her mouth keeps moving after it's stopped saying anything." The manservant looked for acknowledgment, found instead an indecipherable inwardness. He kept on. "Like an echo, but she's mouthing it. Have you noticed that?"

The man stood, glowered, and left the room.

***

He regarded the ground as he knocked. It had all started with that leprous scandal of a door. The man did not want his eyes spoiled by it. There was nothing charming about it, nothing, and she should know that.

And here she was. Her fault, he thought. She knew well how not to answer a door. Remember the day she never answered? Well, she could have done that again, yet here she was, licensing everything that followed.

"It's been some time," she said.

"I hope I'm not burdening you," he said.

"Of course not."

"You should be ashamed of yourself."

"I'm sorry?"

"Yes. What do you know of burdens?? And you the young one, healthy."

She took a step back. "What—Is something wrong?"

"There are many things wrong. But only a coward, a coward-ess, lets that matter." His voice was not raised. He was speaking rather quietly, in fact, and quickly. His was a voice for statistics.

"Life is not a series of perfections," he continued. "You cannot expect perfection. Are you perfect? Your door?" He laughed. "I don't think so. From your mother, from me. Oh love, how terribly inconvenient."

She looked at him a moment.

"You *say* you love me," she said.

"It's me!" Finally he had raised his voice. But it was a pleading voice, as if he were tired of incomprehension. "I'm the one who hates your goddamned door!"

Without indicating the door or anything else, he turned and left.

***

The manservant made her heart a gyroscope.

Each time she opened the door for him, as she faced outward, it beat a happy warmth. The sight of him was healing. She spent so much time thinking of the man that her heart was going sore, just as fingers do when they curl and tighten with nothing to grasp. The manservant's visits were a justifying balm.

But the moment she turned to lead him inside, her heart caved and slid meekly behind her stomach. This was playacting. The manservant said the man did not know he came on these visits. Still. Who did he think he was? The wounded lover? The martyr with an unrequited heartbeat? And she, who was she supposed to be? The unattainable prize? The love-scant shrew, reigning with tantalizing indifference?

Six times the manservant visited.

"It is always a pleasure to see you."

"Thank you, miss. Don't mind me saying, the pleasure is mine."

Six times she pretended not to want to speak of the man.

"And how have you been?"

"Good, good. He misses you, though. He does."

The manservant had a smell. It was tall, bluish, geologic. The man had the same smell.

"What about you?"

"Me?" He looked with alarm at the opposite wall. "I–Of course, yes, I suppose–"

"How have you been, I meant. You, not him."

"Ah, yes, I've been fine." His voice tightened. "Busy. Trying to get away as much as I can. A great time of year for those all-day walks. Not as much as I'd like, though."

"Never as much as we'd like."

The manservant let his lips float apart.

"We're all busier than is good for us," she added, "always too busy."

"Indeed," he said.

The smell contained nothing organic, and resembled the plodding reek of stone, but still it reminded her for some reason of an eagle's wings. Likely it was the castle's scent and their clothing soaked it up.

"The last time he was here, he was—unusual," she said. "Has he spoken of that with you?"

"He is angry with himself, miss. I do not know what happened. He won't tell me. But my feeling? My feeling is it may be one reason he has not returned."

It occurred to her she was being tested. She wanted nothing bad to happen to the man. Yet only an acute and troubling development—an illness, an injury—would support the number of questions she burned to ask about him.

If this was love, she hated it already.

"What are the others?"

"Others?"

"Reasons why he has not returned."

The manservant spoke too glowingly of the man. He took a literal, amateurish approach to his mission. It was hagiography. Oddly, this was effective. She heard enough to miss him. But the frustration in not hearing genuine things, plausible things, left her ravenous when before she'd been merely hungry.

"By coming, he risks you will end it for good. He might knock on your door and you might say it is pointless. He might come to your door and you might never want to see him again. By staying away, there is at least the possibility."

"That is hardly rational."

"It is for someone desperate."

One night she dreamed. The dream was a mass of rectilinear pieces that fit together like teeth. They threw dark shadows, and these fit together, too—an anti-jaw. In the dream everything was precise and had answers. Her fingers, each containing a smaller finger-shaped tube, each in turn containing a tube-shaped answer, flew across the teeth: a keyboard. She looked down but she had no fingers at all. Her arms ended not in hands but in large and intricate devices. She looked up and the sky was the underbelly of a great machine, nippled extravagantly with rivets and bolts. She stood still and the answer in the tube in the right finger of her right hand—fingers again!—was that nose grace, in every circumstance, lasted seven minutes. It was the longest time one could smell burnt toast, or the sweet rot of a corpse, or any smell really, without smelling of it oneself, before it seeped into hair and skin and left a lasting taint. If only she could drop into that castle for seven minutes and fly out of it on the brink of the eighth, she could memorize the scent and have it forever without smelling it on herself, without letting it plague her. A giant eagle, its wings rippling with arrogant muscle, could drop her in and pluck her out just in time.

She heard it. The eagle was outside. It rasped at the door with a single talon. If it lost patience, it might destroy her and her home. Roughly she roused herself.

At the door was the manservant. A seventh visit. He started to say something but saw she was not listening. Her hair was reckless. She did not invite him inside.

"He must prove his devotion," she told the manservant. "Tell him he must give up his wealth."

"You will marry him if he gives up his wealth?"

"If he gives up all his wealth, I will consider it. A 'fundamental virtue' is what he said. He must prove his devotion."

"Must he lose his manservant as well? Not to dwell on selfish concerns."

"Consorting with the possessed does not make you a possession."

"What?"

"No. No, is what I mean to say. His wealth, not you."

The manservant breathed firmly out his nose. His lips were tight with thought, which was why.

"Miss, how will he provide for you both?" he asked, regarding the ground as he asked it.

She brushed this away. "He must prove himself."

As the door closed, the manservant noticed something dragging across his pant leg. It was a green blade of something fernish. He leaned over and gripped the base of the main stalk.

It came out clean, without effort, like an unbarbed arrow from something already dying.

Almost six weeks later the manservant returned. His face was strange.

"It is so good—" she began.

He interrupted. "He has sold everything," he said. "He has nothing. Three days' clothing. A few supplies, including a used canteen but good-quality. And me, of course."

She did not understand.

"He actually did it?" she asked.

"Did what?"

"Gave everything up? His wealth?" Her heart fluttered and plummeted, like a bird full of lead and panic.

"Well, yes. That *is* what you said he should do?"

"No, I said he must. I never said he should." The distinction made sense to her but, she was aware, less so aloud. "Why? Why would he do such a thing?"

The manservant gave the soft smile of someone who had been through this circumstance before—admirable, because of course he hadn't—and who stood ready to reassure.

"He loves you."

"Does he tell you to say that?"

"Who?"

"Him. Does he tell you to say things like that? Or are you improvising?"

The manservant looked at a loss for a moment, then recomposed himself. So completely that he looked satisfied.

"I know it with all my heart, miss. I do."

"Fine," she said, angry. "Fine. How do I even verify this?"

The manservant clasped his hands together and held them toward her.

"Come with me if you'd like. We'll go to the castle. It belongs to the Church now. They've put a young friar in charge. He can confirm it."

If it was true, she resented the religious slant. Was the man mocking her? She looked at the manservant darkly.

"Friar's the hospitable type," the manservant tried. "He'll talk to any breathing soul happens by. Likely has aspirations for parish priest—"

"Indeed, of course. The good friar. A cousin, maybe. From the even more pious side of the family." She did not like herself sarcastic. She felt thirty pounds heavier, jowly. But she couldn't help it. The hot twitching behind her eyes was now in charge.

"And where's Friar's cousin living?" she continued. "No, let me guess. In the castle, I suppose, rent-free as a condition to the sale? Friar likes to play landlord, too, yes?"

"No, miss. He is living in a field. We are. Both of us. Currently."

His clothing did not dispute this. It looked clean enough but rumpled: the uniform of the conscientious poor.

"What about everything else? All his things, his horses?"

The manservant, once so reassuring, now looked in no mood to persuade. He was tired, clearly. The lack of eagerness let her know it was true.

"He gave it away. Well, the money and gold at least. The rest, it was easier to sell off than give for free. Unbelievably suspicious, people. They would rather pay pennies than get at no cost." He sneezed and wiped at nothing with his sleeve. "Then he had to give away the pennies."

She had hoped listening to all of this would put her thoughts right. She had been holding them under this good man's words, waiting for them to wash clean. But she felt worse, not better.

"What am I supposed to do now?"

"Wait, he kept three days' clothing," the manservant said. "Wanted me to make sure you knew that. He's a straight one."

This man hasn't slept in days, she thought.

"Devotion is fine," she found herself saying. "Devotion is virtue. And without ability it amounts to a hole in the empty air. Earn it back."

"Earn what back?"

The manservant was not a contentious man. He genuinely was not understanding her. This made her indignant, made it easier to demand something preposterous.

"All of it. His wealth. His possessions. All of it. Tell him to earn it back. Without ability a man amounts to nothing."

"How is he supposed to do that?"

"That is the question, isn't it?"

The quickness of her own retort reminded her of the man, of that day she awoke to the thump of desultory hail. She had opened the door and stuck her head out. It was him, on her roof, giving her a plain look, as if was there something he could help her with? On the ground was a bucket she did not recognize, stuffed with wet darkness. He was cleaning her gutters.

"What do you think you're doing?" she had asked.

He had crouched at roof's edge, done a little hop, and landed on the ground in the same crouch. Impressive. She had forced herself to consider the film on the rim of the bucket, hoping to hide that she thought so.

"Looking for this," he had said, handing her a leaf. "It took some time. But I finally found it."

So absurd, she'd thought. And she'd kept it.

"Well, what if he can't?" the manservant was now saying.

"He can visit whenever he likes, then as now. But then as now he will not speak of marriage."

"Miss, please. That is not just."

"It is just. Just what I require. Or perhaps he can send me a perfumed note stating he is a man without ability. That way I'll have something to hold to my nostrils when I think of him over the decades."

"He loves you very much," the manservant said. "Very much."

When the manservant turned away silently for the door, she felt sorry, and this provoked her further.

"All of it," she called from the door, as he moved, head down, into the forest.

This manor was wood, not stone. Everywhere she looked, shapes launched themselves from it: towers, dormers, oriels. It had been years since he had given away the castle, and she had never seen it. But she could not imagine it had been more impressive.

Her arrival would cause fanfare. She wished to avoid that until she'd had a chance to see the gifts. She walked the perimeter. There were more doors than she'd anticipated.

At last she chose one on the side, with an open window nearby. Voices, clattering. The protuberant odor of roasting lamb. She'd found the kitchen.

When the door opened, she asked for him by first name. This was a mistake. The fat cook stood there and wiped her hands on her apron, jutting a knowing chin and wiping and wiping.

It was a condemning look. It was a look for a strange woman calling on a man's wedding day, too low or scheming for the main entrance, brandishing a first name. It was the look reserved in this part of the country, she realized, for whores bent on extortion.

"I'm his sister," said the woman. The truth would only delay her.

"Oh! Welcome, welcome!" The cook bustled from the waist up but did not budge. "Of course! Though you wouldn't prefer the main entrance?"

"I know it's early yet. I didn't want to be a bother. I hoped to get a quick word with him before it gets under way in earnest."

"Wait here. Please, sit. Wait here. I'll see if we can't get him."

She sat at a side table. The top was white granite and gleamed. It made her hot hands feel a mess and she took them away. She watched the two remaining cooks. They worked a wall of stoves and ovens. Motion came off them like a spray.

This kitchen alone, she thought.

The one in her home consisted of the yellow stove and the piece of floor under it. It had all started with that square sun of a stove. The air that day had verged on cloud. Once indoors the men had ached to congratulate themselves with stamping and rubbing, but were cowed stiff by strange hospitality. A dog of exquisite alertness. A pot of spiced tea.

This kitchen alone was larger than the only home she'd known.

The cook returned, pink and breathing with her mouth.

"And there she is," she announced.

The man was behind her.

It was shocking how little he'd changed. His hair was still a rich brown. A strand of it wisped across his forehead. She reproved herself for expecting a diminished man, for overestimating her weight on things.

The feeling went away. She was left with a sensation of her abdomen as rubbery ullage. But only for a moment, before it filled with elation.

He stared at her silently. Long enough that the three cooks stared, too. The fat one had time to sit down.

"You're an hour early," he said.

"You're three years late," she said.

He took her by the shoulders. They kissed. She pulled away.

"This is important," she said. "Do not let me be a burden."

He looked at her.

"Now, or later, when we're older. When I'm older. I will not be a burden. To anyone."

He narrowed his eyes and did not let himself smile.

"If you are ever a burden," he said, "I get to carry you with two hands. Not just hold you with one. And my grand plan of three years will have succeeded wildly."

She put a chiding hand against his chest but kissed him a second time. They were making up for the wait.

The fat cook looked scandalized and left.

Again the woman pulled away.

"Take me to the room with the gifts," she said, not looking him in the face.

"The gifts."

"I must see them."

"The wedding gifts?"

"Yes."

"What—You want to see the wedding gifts?" He took his hands down. He had abandoned them in mid-air, in mid-reach, when she'd pulled away.

"I don't want to see them. I must. Now."

The man watched her, his head back a little.

"You are something," he said.

The junior cooks glanced at each other. They were enjoying themselves.

"Had I realized it was a feast that cooked itself," he continued, no more loudly than before, still looking at the woman, "I might have given the kitchen a month off."

Clattering. No voices.

She'd seen the manservant just a week before. It was he who had come to her little house, politely declined to enter, announced the man had earned it all back. A ceremony was being arranged. Perhaps she'd like to attend her own wedding.

He looked exactly a few years older. Under his eyes were dark bands; at last the eyebrows had their reflections. Wrinkles formed like ripples where forehead pooled over nose. Words with the letter "m" sent a hair of coarse silver shivering out a nostril and back in.

Now, at the foot of the stairs on the morning of her wedding day, his words were warm. The rest of him, however, was different. He stood more than straight. He kept his arms at his sides, but tucked his hands back into hiding. And he let her see more of his hands than his eyes.

The man had excused himself for last-minute preparations. The manservant was leading her to the gifts. They took the stairs from the first floor to the third.

"The guests, they're all coming?" she asked.

"Yes, ma'am," he answered, watching his feet take the steps.

"Everyone who was invited?" she asked.

"Yes, everyone, ma'am." He cricked his neck down to look at her, but briefly. "Including, at the bride's request, everyone from whom the groom has profited."

She said nothing.

"Over the last three years." He was smiling. "Because I believe that was her official request?"

Men unused to making light did it too heavily, she thought.

"Was that when she was a ma'am or a miss?" she asked.

"I'm sorry?"

Instantly it was she who was.

"Tell me," she said, "how have you been?"

"I've been fine, fine," he said. "I'm fine. You?"

"In a daze, frankly." She coughed once; a small laugh, but this was clear only after it finished.

When they reached the third floor, he took her to a set of double doors and opened them.

She did not look inside. She looked down the hallway, where something moved.

It was Basil. He was portly now, a furry trolley. Skinny legs but flanks so excessive they continually arranged themselves as the legs made progress.

He sniffed the floor, making as if he had no particular anxiety to see her. But he let himself steal looks. And each bat of his tail brought rump with it.

She milked his ears. He wet the floor. She scritched his snout. He raised a genial leg after the fact.

When Basil opened his eyes again, she straightened. She looked past the double doors into the room. This is what she saw:

Stacks of fine count linen; a bronze candelabra on the floor; its twin squatting on a harpsichord bench; the harpsichord itself, an old thing, its ivory keyboard scrimshawed with a mural of a forest scene, its high D a dryad involving herself with a woodsman; a French duck press; two sets of dyed velvet drapes, one indigo, the other cochineal, draped over a rocking horse like a mane that a unicorn might shake his head at; a man's watch fastened frivolously around a string of pearls; an armoire with his initial carved in the left door and hers in the right, barely legible for all the finials; a mahogany serving table; resting on top of it (and perched near a corner as if considering flight) a brooch in the shape of a butterfly; a set of seventy-three volumes, each a book of the Bible, bound in what she was sure was lambskin; four lamps (two lit) wearing stained-glass shades that ignited their paneled colors but threw whitest light; three suits of armor; Luxembourgeois china, settings and settings, showing hand-painted vines and leaves mingling as in nature with shoots and blooms embroidered in gold along undulating circumferences; a roll-top desk quiet as a blinking eye; a silver trumpet; a crystal cask.

Beyond these, farther into the room, there was more. It was overwhelming.

"I think I've seen enough," she said to the manservant.

"You don't need to see the other rooms then?"

"Other rooms?"

She followed as he showed her the rest. Every room on the floor was littered with treasure. Every room was an opportunity for Basil to wreath his big body around it all. Somehow he knew to slap his tail against the sturdy objects and not the fragile.

The dog's glee proved convenient. She used it to mask her indifference, observing its duration as a measure for waiting and pretending to admire.

For really she cared little about these objects except as evidence. They showed the man's goodness to the people with whom he'd dealt. Other inferences were possible, no doubt. The gifts could mean merely that he was being cultivated for future business. But the nature of these items—considered, idiosyncratic, warmly generous—suggested otherwise.

He had proven his character.

The ceremony started promptly at noon. It lasted a good time, because talking was the friar's favorite. The groom and bride showed the same questionable discipline as Basil, stealing looks by turn while the other paid attention.

He thought about her cheekbones, how his lips wanted to take care of them.

She thought about the wisp of hair that floated over his forehead, how she could hang on it all her misgivings.

At the end he kissed her. She looked flushed.

"Are you all right?" he asked. "Do you need anything?"

"Nothing at all," she said, moving that wisp of hair back into place, because she did not need it.

The receiving line was a blur. With all the people, her head whipped this way and that. She took a hand and discovered the fat cook on the end of it.

"It's not right, you know," said the cook who, grimacing, gave the captive forearm a quick rap and moved on.

***

They spent the night in the manor. The next morning they slept in, ate, did little that mattered.

The boredom got to her. She was anxious to get outside, take a day trip somewhere. She reminded him she needed to get her things, from her old house.

"Love is lazy," he said. "Love reclines."

"So lazy it proposes fifty times," she said, running a fingertip across his lower lip, "and cleans gutters."

He prevailed and stayed on the sofa. She got up and went to the other side of the room.

"Whose gift was this?" she asked, sitting down at the harpsichord.

"Don't know," he said, lighting a pipe. "I don't remember it arriving, actually."

A few keys stuck. A low F sharp was silent altogether. But the sound was like winter sun, precise and beautiful.

He blew rings to match the mood of the music. Carefree at first, the shapes of the rings changed right away and continued to change: uncertain, inquisitive, surprised, delighted. She'd continued playing even after making her discovery. The scrimshaw on the keyboard crept down the sides of keys. The hidden carvings were like secrets stuck between feasting teeth, showing only when adjacent notes were pressed. They kept the mural whole, seamless, as the instrument was played. But they also amplified it, adding new scenes, new details of scenes, with each sound. There was a boy who, having just sold his hands to a witch, held the purchase money in his teeth; a hunter walking on the tops of trees with the slack carcass of a cloud over his shoulder; a needle-fanged infant of a porcupine hatching from a pinecone; a naked man crouching and blowing into the trunk of a tall tree perforated along its height with seven bird-sized holes; seven birds, some landing on the holes and some flitting just off of them, directed by an elaborately gowned woman using a disembodied beak to conduct; a fisherman caught by the boot between two rocks at the top of an enormous cataract, his basket blown to bits in the churn below; a river flowing into the front door of a cabin in whose second-story window an empty rowboat was just visible; a mother with triplet babies, two suckling at her breasts and the third on the knob of her anklebone.

She remembered the young lovers. There they were, on high D. She played them and leaned to inspect what their neighbor was hiding.

On the near side of high E was the same nymph from D, but older, and wearing something dark. A black dress? The somber figure held with her fingertips the edges of the gown falling off her younger rapturing D-self and flowing from the face of one key up the side of the next.

The widow was not gazing directly at the lovers embracing. Nor was she looking down. She was staring away, at a point in space above the middle of the keyboard. She'd been carved to look the player of the instrument in the face. Her expression—though tinily rendered—was recognizable. It was not the look of remembering, but of considering what might have been.

"It is beautiful," he said.

She gave a start. "What?"

He was looking out the window. "Outside. It's a wonderful day."

He was talking, she realized, because she had stopped playing.

"Someone should experience it before it ends," she said.

She joined him where he sat. An hour later, wife and husband for exactly a day, they chastised each other happily for having done nothing about going outdoors. Finally the man found the manservant to fit out the horse and buggy.

"Maybe the carriage instead?" the manservant suggested, rather woodenly. "I'll drive and let the two of you enjoy." He glanced nervously at the woman and back at the man.

"The buggy's fine," said the man. "We'll make up for our idle morning."

It had not rained in a while. The ground made for smooth riding—no mud, no debris from wind or rain. Above, equally perfect. The sky was packed blue dirt. They wandered for hours.

Just after they turned to head home, they passed under a series of low boughs. The man stood impulsively and snatched at a leaf. At the same moment the buggy lurched to the right. He nearly fell out.

Sitting back down, he gave her the leaf.

"The twin I've been looking for," he announced.

"Put up quite a fight, didn't it?" she said.

"It is fierce," he said. "Know that it may not survive in captivity."

They returned at sunset. The manor not yet visible, they saw smoke. The woman's head went clear with alarm. As they got closer, the man noted the smoke was not pouring freely. It was the traipsing smoke of a fire already extinguished.

They arrived. A jagged smoldering pile. Where the manor should have been.

Their home had burned to the ground.

One lump on the grass was different from the rest: an island off a mainland of devastation. It was the silhouette of a dog. Basil had his head on his paws, his lids half-closed against the smoke but his eyes alert.

The woman stood there, both hands on her head, staring.

"What's happened?" she asked the man.

The man said nothing. The manservant, who had been working on the far side of the property, made his way over.

"What's happened?" the woman asked the manservant.

The manservant approached but said nothing.

"Why is the ground wet?" the woman asked again.

It was all too much to fathom. She would get command of one thing at a time. She wondered why the man wasn't saying anything.

"No need for the grass to die," said the manservant.

"Where were you?" she asked him.

"Here, right here."

"I–" the man interjected, but the woman did not let him finish.

"Are you all right?" she asked the manservant.

"Perfectly."

"Why is the ground wet?"

"I dampened it before starting the fire. In a circle, to keep the flames close. No need for the grass to die."

"You started the fire?" she asked.

"Yes."

The woman looked at the man, then back at the manservant.

"*You* started this fire?"

The manservant looked at the man uncertainly and opened his mouth, and the man opened his mouth, and before either spoke the woman took two quick steps and put the heel of her hand in the manservant's face.

It landed hard under his nose, as if she meant to take it off. The manservant fell back and lay on the ground and did not move. He blinked, but did not move.

Gently the man helped her victim up, brushed the nettles out of his hair. The man looked over at the woman—warily, admiringly—as he did so.

And then he explained everything.

The four of them walked the ruins. They took shallow breaths because the smoke was still sharp.

The woman walked alone. They had burned her little house, too. The man had done it himself, after she'd arrived on the morning of the ceremony. He told her this with the face of a man swallowing glass. She wanted to hit him anyway. But she had no more violence in her, and instead withdrew.

She considered the man's reasoning. She had proven her character. She had put fantastic will behind a desire for a worthy man.

Her ability, too. She had secured him finally, and on precisely her terms.

But not her devotion, the man pointed out. Not yet.

They were penniless. They had nothing in the world. Except two animals and a serviceable buggy.

If she stayed with this man, it would be because she had to. It would be a ransom for cruelty. It would be the kind of devotion a beating brings. But who was she to call cruelty, she who had played with another man's life with pigtail petulance? If she left this man, it would be for spite—an abandonment for two arsons. It was likely not the worst reason to do something, but maybe the least principled given all she'd burn down doing it.

She looked up. Man and manservant were circling the property. They picked their way slowly, gazing down, grimly. She had not seen anyone move like this; it was the walk of people in a graveyard who knew all the buried.

He was wrong. For him, it was a test of devotion. For her, devotion had nothing to do with it. She craved that man's face and hands, her sweetest concern was what he would say next, the air she liked best had the damp of his breath in it.

He must have felt relief when she flattened the manservant, she thought. Likely he'd feared her reaction and believed that was the worst of it. Part of her wanted to devise something worse, something subtle and brilliant and obvious only in retrospect. But she was not that kind of person.

She could not remember with clarity the kind of person she'd been before. Who would she be after?

Devotion was beside the point. But character. What kind let itself be subjugated? What kind destroyed itself so it could say it had not been subjugated?

What had seemed a long time was seven minutes. Seven minutes in that reprehensible smoke was all the woman needed to decide.

She stayed. Even though he had taken from her everything in the world.

She did.

She stayed with him. Nothing else in the world mattered.

For a night they camped in the woods. For a day they went around with only the clothes they wore. The manservant stayed behind with horse, buggy, and dog. One of these looked hungry.

"What do we do now?" asked the man, as he and the woman walked up their seventh hillside.

"Go to the city?"

"Maybe."

"Or not."

"Maybe deeper into the country. Where seeing another human being is a surprise."

She grabbed his hand. "Yes, surprise. From another human being. I haven't had much of that lately."

They returned. Basil was asleep. Nothing else had changed. The man asked the manservant to fit out the buggy and horse. He ignored the woman's inquiring eyebrows.

They got in. The dog cocked back his whole body with arthritic preciousness before taking two hops—to floor, to seat—and wedged himself between them. He did not care where his flankmeat fell. The manservant rode standing, single-footed on the side step opposite from the man.

"Where are we going?" she asked.

The man took the reins.

"Deeper into the country. You said so."

He gave the reins a snap. Basil gave the air a yelp.

They skirted the valley, cut through a peninsula of forest, and emerged into a clearing. Near the center stood two enormous oaks. Each had dropped an extraordinary acorn. Or so it seemed to the woman, giddy from not having eaten. One was in the shape of a modest home, the other a full-sized barn.

The front door to this home, like the rest of it, was freshly painted. The man asked the manservant to open it. He did. The man entered and waited for her inside.

"What is this?" she asked.

The house was small enough that the man could afford it after selling most of the gifts, and large enough that it fit the rest of them. The broker had found it in less than a week. This was half the time the same broker had taken, and so discreetly, with an earlier request from the manservant: a harpsichord, ancient but hardwearing, for two chandeliers.

On her way in, she could think of nothing clever, and simply smoothed a wisp of his hair with a hand that trembled.

"What's in there?" She pointed at one of the rooms.

"Occupied," said the man.

"By whom?"

"Your things. From your house. Before I—before it went—"

She flicked her handkerchief up at him. She'd been using it for her eyes. It landed on his cheek softly, as if forgiveness had intervened.

"I should stay close," she said. "If I turn around, you might burn them."

They repaired to their bedrooms for the night, the couple upstairs, the manservant on the first floor, near the door.

Before going to bed, the man went for a walk outside. It was cold but he did not bring a coat. He saw near the door of this small new home the beginning of a dogstile. It did not quite reach across the door. It would in time.

Before going to bed, the woman sat down at the harpsichord. She ran her fingers lightly over the keys in mute glissandos. Things rippled in and out of view. Her fingers did not feel like they contained answers at all. She put two of them on the notes on either side of the high D, and pushed in and down. The square front edge bore painfully into the soft web between her fingers. For the first time the sides of the high D were revealed. On the near side was a picture of the woodsman's boots. He had taken them off before commencing. One was tumbled over on its side, the other still upright though half-buried under its fallen brother. The boots did not match; peeking from the top of the standing one was the fleeting tip of a snake's tail. On the far side of the same key was another addendum to the lovers' scene—just the woman's forearm and hand, wandering out in mid-air and hanging free of everything else. The fingers were curiously depicted. They were neither calm nor tightly closed, but outstretched, wavering in half-rigid extension. And then she remembered the widow on the adjacent side of the next key up. The young woman was holding her hand out toward her. Perhaps the woman was reaching to herself. Perhaps she was already conscious in mid-experience that she would remember. Or that years later even the memory of the longing would not have gone away.

The manservant was exhausted from doing things he had never done before: systematically emptying a house, systematically burning it, giving up his seat to a dog. He stayed in and dreamed.

Just before dawn the woman awoke. She heard a noise, noises, like whining or crying. The man still slept. She dressed quickly and went downstairs.

It was Basil. He was at the manservant's door, scratching furiously, moaning. She stood to the side. She did not want to get in the way of all that dog.

She knocked. Emboldened, the dog began to bark. No answer came. She pushed the door open.

There, not in the barn, or from one of the oaks outside, but in the close humility of his new adopted room, hung the manservant, from a squat rope looking of wizened wood.

The body was pure weight. The cord, stiff from strain, was too short. She refused to consider this. It meant a slow choking.

Only years later, there in the same house, smaller for three children and an obese dog, did it occur to her to look. It had been so long since she'd touched the instrument. Always too busy. The key stood out starkly now, the high C, the next key down from the affair. The top of it was provocative in its blandness, showing only a few clouds. The house was all hush and cool spaces; children down for a rare nap, man and dog ignorant of this and out hunting their own quiet. She sat. The lovers sank down in their throes. She rose again, keeping her finger there. She shifted from the center of the keyboard to the other side of them. She looked back over the tangled bodies at their neighbor, that little wall of wood ledged with ivory. She did these things and felt the stun of too many implausibilities: that she had never looked before; that she had no idea what it would show; that she believed it could mean anything. It was her guess, her hope, that the scale of it would be too small for rendering the entirety of that foolish, wandering, sunwashed day, that day spent in the woods, three days after their first meeting, when the manservant had tried to kiss her—no, he had kissed her—after calling her miss. It would be too small to show her mouthing the word, without thinking about it, its first letter perfect for a kiss.

It was the woodsman, alone. He carried a smoking torch and walked into the hills. One of these was marked like a scar by the shadow of an eagle overhead. He looked over his shoulder at himself and his love, the scene indeed small, his face smaller still, his eyes impossible at this scale to depict, but his brows solemn and their reflections, too, a man considering what should have been.

ACKNOWLEDGMENTS

I WANT TO THANK DAVID LEAVITT AND ROXANE GAY. THEY PUB-lished my earliest work. They showed faith and gave encouragement when neither was in evident supply. "It's beautifully written," David wrote in the first acceptance I ever received, "very sad, very funny, and—how else to put it?—about so much more than it appears to be about." Here's how to put it, David: thank you for keeping me going.

Thanks also to the editors of the magazines and anthologies in which some of these stories first appeared: "Troth," *Michigan Quarterly Review* 52, no. 4 (2013), republished in *New Millennium Writings* (2015) as the winning story for the New Millennium Fiction Prize; "94 Selvage Street #1," *Chautauqua* 12; "How Héctor Vanquished the Greeks," *Harvard Review Online* (2015); "Pleasantville," *Alaska Quarterly Review* 33, nos. 1–2 (2016); "The Duplex and the Scarp," *Witness* 29, no. 2 (2016); "John Tan Can't Play Classical Guitar,"

Subtropics 16 (2013); "Kennedy Travel," *The Southern Review* 51, no. 3 (2015); "The Girl Who Not Once Cried Wolf," *Mid-American Review* 35, no. 1 (2014); "You Will Excuse Me," *Los Angeles Review* 15 (2014), republished in *The Best Small Fictions 2015*; and "On the Far Side of the Sea," *PANK* 8, no. 9 (2013), republished as a featured selection in *Longform.org* (2013), *Paragraph* 55 (2014), and *Paragraph Shorts* (2014).

I need to thank Paul Kim and Jodi Zisser. They are great friends and great fans. I don't deserve what they give me. But I'll take it. George Burchill has inspired and encouraged for decades now, and he must know that this, here, is the only time I will ever call him George. And of course there is the actual and estimable John Tan, who would give me the name off his back.

How to thank CeCe and Bill Kane? For their strength and their cheer and their wisdom, and for the sheer privilege of knowing them and learning from them, and for the stupid pleasure of enjoying life in their company. All the things they do so generously give me the time and the space to write, and so—in a real way—this book was written by them.

Finally, for Cathy Kane, there is no thanking. Only worship. This is the word for what one gives in return for everything.